Cameo's twin sister Camille receives a good dose of much overdue karma. What she does with it is even more destructive than her previous betrayal. The woman is a maneater with no conscience.

Cameo takes off in her car after Rush tries to play the dominance card. While she's away, a call from the past reveals unbelievable news! Her life is about to change directions in a big way, and only one man might have the compass she needs to move forward.

Rebar and Cameo share a tender moment, indicating that a reconciliation may be in their distant future. That is, if another man doesn't get in the way again.

In the Middle
Copyright © 2023 Shiloh Love
ISBN: 978-1-4874-4055-8
Cover art by Martine Jardin

Published by eXtasy Books Inc

Look for us online at:
www.eXtasybooks.com

# In the Middle
# Feather Blue 8

## By

## Shiloh Love

# CHAPTER ONE

"I tried," Malika said while gazing at her reflection in the mirror and unraveling the braid in her long black hair. "I didn't expect to encounter such fierce opposition from Shook."

"We can't give up," Shade said. "Ricochet will be punished."

"I know that. You know that. But convincing Cameo is another story. She's always been an independent thinker. Joan and Missy would've never been able to blackmail her. We can't move forward until Cameo is onboard with us." Malika turned to face him, clad in a sheer black negligée slit up both sides to her hip, with a V-neck that plunged to her perfect navel. "How do you like this one? Am I not the most alluring woman you've ever seen?"

He reached out and grabbed her slender waist, pulling her toward him as he sat on the edge of the bed. "Indeed you are." His lips skimmed the bare skin of her midriff. "And I've waited long enough."

She straddled his bare lap. "It's been a long week. Put out this fire that's consuming me, then we can talk more."

"Wicked wench," he growled against her skin. "Using your daughters to further your agenda."

"If I can get Cameo and Camille in the same corner, Ricochet won't stand a chance." She gasped as he thrust into her. "I almost had her . . ." She threw her head back as pleasure ripped through her. "She's still on the fence . . ." Malika let out a long moan.

"Shut up, woman, and enjoy the ride." He rolled her onto his huge bed and stared down at her. "Does your brain ever stop?"

"No . . ." she replied on an airy breath, then cried out as he took her hard.

No man could match his prowess in bed. He pleased her, satisfied her every kinky urge and crazy needs. She closed her eyes as he bit her neck. Her nails raked the rippling muscles of his back, then dug in, silently demanding he increase his pace. She wound her long legs around his lower back, panting next to his ear as his sweat-beaded body moved against hers.

They made wild, frenzied love for at least an hour, she guessed, peaking several times at the time, before collapsing on the bed. He lay panting beside her for a while before speaking.

"No woman has ever done me like you do, Malika. Don't even think of breaking things off with me, no matter what happens with your girls."

"Ah, Shade," she mused with an airy laugh. "You worry too much. You know I'd never give up a stud like you. After all, I did promise Tassos I'd give his sons the best."

A deep laugh rumbled in his chest. "You think Tassos would care? You know the truth now. I'm not Greek. I'm just one hundred percent stud."

"That you are." She turned her head to look at him. "You now know the truth about me as well, yet you still want me in your bed."

"I'm willing to overlook your lunatic, narcissistic, malicious, personalities if they benefit me. I know a good thing when I see it." He shifted onto his side. His seductive dark eyes pierced her soul. "Maybe you even did me a favor. The General was old and getting overbearing. I no longer have to do his bidding, thanks to you," he murmured near her ear, then bit the lobe causing her to squeal.

2

"You're not even a little angry that I killed your father and stepsister?" Malika let her hand glide over his huge bicep.

He dropped a kiss on her lips. "Nah. The General was a sick bastard. You put him out of everyone's misery, just as you did Jared. You're an unpredictable dangerous vixen, but I love you anyway."

"Mm. And I love you too, darling. Strong, virile, gorgeous, and practical like me. Looks like you're running the show now. You're the new kingpin, Shade Damocles."

"Correction," he stated. "Trenton Shade. Damocles was a perfect cover while I needed one. I fear the cat's outta the bag now since you told Cameo."

"Perhaps just a little. But Cameo is not a chatterbox. I sensed conflict in her during that last dance at the old Indian's cabin. She wants to believe her mother is not what everyone says. There's a little glitch, though."

"What's that?"

"Her feelings for Rebar. She's not over him so we can't send Camille after Rebar again to find his device. That was a bad idea. It caused more dissension between the girls. I need them to join forces before we dismantle Ricochet. I want them on our side and Camille is the key."

"Too bad. I came up with the perfect plan. I surely thought Rebar and Camille would hook up, and Cameo would move on. Then we wouldn't have to sneak around this way." He sighed in open frustration. "Actually, Cameo did move on. It was that jerkoff Rebar who didn't move on. Had he just done the right thing and stuck with Camille, I'd have let him off the hook for his betrayal of us. But now he must pay."

"All of Ricochet has to pay. We also underestimated Shook. He knew how to use the dance against me. He combined his Lakota Medicine with Cameo's Lakota blood and severed the connection I had established. I've lost my edge." She growled. "He's FBI, you know."

"Then I guess you should stay out of his way."

Malika narrowed her eyes. "I fear no man. Shook just put himself in my crosshairs. He betrayed me. Tricked me. I never suspected he was a Fed. He'll be sorry he ever messed with me."

"We'll take Ricochet down together, my love." He nipped at her fingertips as they traced his lips. "I'm more determined than ever to destroy Rebar. Can't believe he got the drop on me. Camille sure blew that mission to hell."

"She did." Malika half frowned. "I thought surely she'd pull it off. After all, she got you."

"Ha, funny. I didn't enjoy your blackmail scheme with Joan and Missy. But . . ." He lifted his brows. "It did get us together and I don't regret that. Gotta give Camille credit, though. She really held it together and saved my life while those wackos you recruited chased us through the bayou."

"Yes, she was strong back then. However, she isn't woman enough to hold your heart."

"She would've been had I not met you. Ah, either way, the moment you walked up to me in the compound, my path was set. I tried to forget you, tried to be happy with Camille. But I couldn't. Never have I met a woman with more fire and ice. I had to have you."

"We can't ever let Camille find out about us," Malika pressed a perfectly manicured finger to his lips in a gesture of hush. "I worked hard getting her to forgive me and reconcile. And I'm awfully close to winning Cameo over. Once I have both my girls, we can bring them to our side and crush Ricochet."

"Rebar just keeps getting in the way," Shade grumbled. "First his sneaky tracking, then both your daughters smitten with him, and now he's sided with those renegades. They'll have access to all his tracking devices. That technology was supposed to be mine once Rebar perfected it."

"He is a problem." She sighed. "Now Rush and Shook are complications, too. They are drawn to Cameo. How do I get her away from Ricochet? A reconciliation between the girls seems impossible."

Shade dipped one brow. "Not according to Camille. She told me that Cameo was very forgiving, that they shared a moment, whatever that means. I was under the impression they've reached a milestone."

"Really? How interesting." She pondered his words for a moment. "Did Camille say anything conclusive?"

"According to her, Cameo said all was forgiven. They shared a hug. Everything was moving in the right direction until Camille approached Rebar. Sounded like some claws came out. But in the end, Cameo expressed interest in getting together and Camille kind of blew her off."

"Anything else? Some minor detail we can build on?" she pushed.

"Geez, woman. Making me think so hard after ravaging my body." He laughed. "We're supposed to be enjoying some afterglow here."

Malika rolled on top of him, positioning her body readily over his. "I'll give you all the afterglow you can handle once we come up with a plan. Now think."

Shade got quiet, simply staring up at her. She felt his arousal again and marveled at the man's stamina. But unless he racked that brain of his, she'd tease him into agony then leave him burning for the night.

His eyes widened with enlightenment. "Camille sounded jealous. She mentioned how Cameo had eight men wrapped around her finger and not an ugly one in the bunch. She complained about her sister's shameful flirting with an entire pack of bikers. She also mentioned how protective they seemed of her."

"Ah-ha. I knew if I went through the right channel your

memory would sharpen." Malika smirked. "And they say the way to a man's heart is through his stomach." She deliberately rubbed against him in all the right places. "I beg to differ."

He blew out a breath. "We're good to go now?"

"I do believe we've found an angle into the heart of Ricochet. Pierce its heart and the beast will fall."

Shade narrowed his eyes. "What do you have in mind?"

"Encourage Camille to seek out her sister for that tentative get together. Cameo's forgiving nature won't change, she's always been the nice one. Once Camille gets a taste of her twin's world of men, she'll want some of that and be more agreeable toward her sister. Two stunning women, three available men . . . a surefire recipe for inner conflict. We'll simply sit back and let human nature take over as Ricochet implodes, then pluck them one-by-one like sitting ducks."

"Use the girls as tools without telling them," Shade said with a grin. "I'd like nothing more than to watch Ricochet lose everything, especially since Rebar took half my team with him."

"Victory is on the horizon. You work on Camille, get her to reconcile with her sister. I'll continue seeking Cameo's trust. I know Cameo is not serious about Rush yet. I saw her flirting with Shook. My lovely twins just may be Ricochet's weak spot."

"There's a flaw in your plan. Camille will still be in our way."

She flashed him a hot look. "You don't think my beautiful Camille can seduce one of those road rats? They aren't all in love with Cameo."

"Yeah. So. What if she does? No guarantee she can get one to the altar."

"You think like a man." Malika flattened both hands against his bare chest and pushed him down on the bed. "The tryst with Rebar was orchestrated by us, which may be the reason it failed. Maybe Camille's heart wasn't invested. She may have sensed you were pushing her away. This time, we take a different approach. Nudge Camille toward her sister, not a man."

"Ohhh, reverse psychology."

She rolled her eyes slightly. "I knew you'd catch on. When I had Camille blackmailed to abduct you, I set it up so that you'd be the victim. I knew she'd fall for you on her own. If you can persuade Camille to spend more time with her sister, the potent allure of those men, combined with a growing sisterhood bond, will be more powerful than her engagement to you. And even if she doesn't break it off, you can end it when you find out she was unfaithful."

"Ah, so this plan is failsafe. You've got us covered either way."

"Yes, my gorgeous stud. And once your engagement is off, you can move me in as queen of your castle. A strong king needs an invincible queen at his side."

"That you are."

"Did you know that my name means queen in Arabic?" She flashed a haughty smile.

"It fits." He lifted her hand and kissed the palm. "What's your plan once Camille has wormed her way into Ricochet?"

"Rip Ricochet's heart right out from under them by taking the girls into hiding. That's where your men come into action. Rush and his group will be blindsided and full of mistrust, conflict. Their infrastructure will weaken. With their jugular exposed, revenge will be ours."

Apprehension crossed his rugged face. "And what if the girls decide to side with Ricochet?"

"They are much too intelligent to bind themselves to road rats. Once they realize we are the strongest force, they'll lose interest in those common rebels."

"And on the off chance they don't? What then?"

"Then we'll crush them, along with the unworthy men they choose." Malika stiffened over his doubt. "You'd best hire exemplary men that can carry out my plan and keep my daughters safely hidden while we finish off Ricochet . . . one man at a time . . . starting with Shook. There won't be anything left of Ricochet for the girls to go back to when we're done. But for your sake, Trenton Shade, your men better not fail because it would not bode well for you to disappoint me."

His gaze shifted from questioning to heated. "And you'd be well off not to dissatisfy me. I'm tired of waiting to have you full-time."

She smiled at his challenge and loved how he never bowed to anyone. His fire made her want him even more.

She wondered if ever forced to choose, would she choose her beautiful daughters or this dangerously irresistible man who satisfied her every desire?

The decision wouldn't be that tough if Camille and Cameo failed her again. Malika wasn't sure she could give up this hunk of man who oozed sexual charisma. Shade had no fear of her. They'd met while he was chained to a pole at her command, yet the man pursued her anyway. He didn't seem bothered by their eleven-year age difference either.

He was the only man she deemed worthy of her love.

"Are we done talking yet, woman?" He rolled her onto her back.

"Yes." She glanced at the clock on his bureau. "We've got less than an hour before Camille returns from that class she's taking. Make it good."

He shifted her into a more feral position. "Don't I always."

She laughed lightly then muffled a scream in his bed pillow as he gave her what she needed.

While in the throes of untamed heated passion, the bedroom door burst open. Malika didn't bother to look up. Her mind blurred on the edge of ecstasy. Whoever had barged in on them would have to wait a few more seconds, just a few more seconds.

"Mother! Shade!"

The door slammed against something hard, and the sound of breaking glass jarred Malika from bliss.

Shade froze in position kneeling behind her. Malika turned her head sideways to see Camille glaring at them, her face wet with tears.

"How could you?" Camille cried.

Malika untangled herself and crawled off the bed. "We weren't expecting you home for another ten minutes or so . . ." She panted for breath and stole a glimpse at the clock.

"Obviously." Camille's eyes flashed with ire as she turned them on Shade. "You lying cheating bastard!"

"Don't blame him, darling. I needed a shoulder to lean on after Ricochet betrayed me. Shade gave me a sympathetic ear and emotional support."

"Support?" Camille shrieked. "That's not all he's giving you!"

"Now, now, calm down. You and I have come so far, and your sister is softening toward us. Don't blow this out of proportion and ruin the progress we've made." Malika tried to sound rational.

"You call this progress, huh?" Camille seethed through clenched teeth.

Shade finally spoke up. "This is the first time, babe. Your mother needed a—"

"Save it!" Camille glanced at the floor. "Traveling light while on the run, Malika?" She kicked the slinky negligée with her boot. "I can't even wrap my mind around this. You killed Shade's brother, his father, and the General's daughter, yet here you are in bed with each other?" Her furious gaze went back to Shade. "You're the General's son and never told me?"

"My father was a private man. He had his reasons. I couldn't break his trust."

"Trust? Trust?" Her voice hitched. "You're having an affair with m-m-my mother. You don't know the meaning of the word."

"It's not as bad as it seems," Shade told her. "We were talking. She started crying. And things just went too far."

Camille grabbed a vase from the dresser and whipped it at Shade, clipping the side of his head before the vase smashed against the headboard. Chards of glass sprayed across the bed.

"How stupid do you think I am? I've been sitting outside this door for over an hour listening to the two of you. It took everything in me not to storm in earlier, but I needed to hear the truth. And that I did. I heard everything . . . all of it."

"Then you know we only want the very best for you and your sister," Malika appealed to Camille's logic.

"You're both sickening!" She twisted her engagement ring off her finger and flung it onto the bed. "My class was canceled today. I was in the garage when I glanced out the window and saw Malika on the porch. You weren't exactly discreet when you greeted each other with a kiss. Guess you thought nobody was around. I waited a few minutes, then came in. Didn't take long to figure out where you were." She let out a scream of rage then cleared the dresser with a sweep of her arm.

Cologne bottles, an antique wash basin, and a mix of other items crashed to the floor. Camille swung back around with such rage on her face, Malika feared she might shoot them with the gun Shade kept in his top drawer.

"Camille, please calm down. You're going to have a break-down," Malika pleaded, keeping her eyes on that top drawer.

Camille's gaze followed Malika's. She opened the drawer and looked inside then lifted the .45 caliber pistol from within.

"This what you're worried about?" She pulled the hammer back and took aim. "That I might shoot you?" She let out a short sardonic laugh. "I suppose you *would* think that given your history." She pulled the trigger.

Malika screamed and dove off the bed. Shade seemed frozen in shock with his back pressed against the headboard. More glass shattered as Camille shot at the windows, the mirrors, and emptied the magazine into everything around them. When the shooting stopped, Malika peeked up over the bed.

"Don't worry, Malika. Your boytoy is still alive. I may not be the *nice one* but I'm not batshit crazy like you." And with that, Camille threw the empty weapon at them, spun, and bolted from the room.

"Should we go after her?" Shade asked.

"No. This is perfect. Camille will run straight to Ricochet, just like we want."

"You planned this, didn't you?"

"I'll never tell." Malika smirked. "I'd better leave. She may call the police. Or Shook. I'm a wanted woman."

Shade looked at her, still seemingly dazed. "Have you forgotten who I am? I'm the General's son. You're not going anywhere."

# CHAPTER TWO

Cameo and Rush rolled into Dallas just after dark. She whispered a prayer of thanks as the four Harleys slowed and veered onto Rush's mile-long driveway of his massive ranch. The ride from South Dakota back to Texas had been much more enjoyable than their trip up. No tornadoes this time, only sunny blue skies and temps in the mid-eighties, perfect August biking weather.

She'd seen half of Ricochet in their natural element while visiting Shook's Native American father at the remote cabin in Pine Ridge. These men were tough and knew how to live off the land. They didn't bow to fear in any circumstance even when tornadoes roared past the motel.

Spending a few days with White Wolf had given her the privilege of feeling her Lakota heritage through a genuine Medicine Man. She found much of the culture peaceful and akin to nature while other aspects were a bit too primitive to her liking. Dancing around the fire was one of the most liberating experiences of her life, especially the first dance. The second, more ritualist dance, had terrified her when Malika's alter *Feather Blue* joined in. Cameo never wanted to go through anything like that again.

She wondered where her mother was now and about her state of mind. Ricochet had yet again vowed to help Malika as long as hope existed.

As they pulled up to the house, Cameo saw the other half of Ricochet come trotting around the corner of the house to the garage. They must've been hanging out waiting for someone to show up. All four men bore worried expressions.

Moss stalked over to Rush before they even dismounted. "Where the hell have y'all been?" His Texas drawl was more evident when worried. "Earlier this week I received strange texts from Halo, then nothing. What'd you do, drop off the face of the Earth for a week?"

Rush calmly parked the bike and slid off, then helped Cameo off. "We rode up to see a Medicine Man," he replied as if it were nothing out of the ordinary.

"Say what?" Moss's brows shot up. "Who? Where?"

"Shook's father. It's a long story. Let us get settled and we'll fill you in," Rush told him.

Stoke, Rider, and Shook parked their bikes, then everyone followed Rush into the house. He dropped their bags on the floor, grabbed cold drinks from the fridge, and led the group out to the patio.

She looked from one man to the other, settling her gaze lastly on Rebar who stood several feet away from the pack. He looked rough. His hair was no longer wavy and freshly styled as usual but disheveled with long bangs over his dark eyes — eyes that carried shadows of hard days.

Her focus zeroed in on the cross necklace around his neck then back to his eyes. He stared back at her with intense, yet visibly mixed emotions. She glanced at Rush who was settling in with the guys then she looked back at Rebar and noticed bruises and scrapes on his face and arms.

Reflexively, her hand covered her mouth as tears formed in her eyes. She tilted her head just slightly in outward compassion. She took a few steps toward him, and he did the same. They closed the gap quickly.

"Aw . . . look at you," she murmured in a shaky voice, then rested one hand alongside his cheek. "What happened?"

"Ran into a couple storms." He sounded aloof.

"The tornado?"

"That and another thing." A haunted past saturated his smoky eyes. "Moss said you texted him that we were trapped in my car. How'd you know?"

"Long story. Are you okay?" She searched his eyes. He seemed so lost. "What was the other thing?"

"Longer story," he countered.

She grasped that he'd closed himself off to her, maybe to everyone, as was his style when he suffered from inner turmoil. Sorrow deluged her to see him this way. Gingerly, she lifted the cross.

"Where'd you get this?"

"You're just full of questions today, aren't ya?" He gave her a pointed look.

"Sorry." She relented. "I don't like seeing you this way."

"Which way?" He cocked one brow.

"Defeated."

Her hand rested on his chest. He wrapped his hand around it. "You didn't answer me, kitten. How'd you know we were trapped?"

She was shocked that he called her *kitten*. She remembered telling him never to call her that pet name again. Yet in this moment, she didn't want to hurt him further.

"This will sound crazy," she began, not pulling her hand away. "But my mother found me and told me you were trapped. I have no idea how she knew. I texted Moss right away and told him."

"Why?"

She gasped in surprise. "You really need to ask?" Tears slid down her cheeks. It ripped her apart to see him this way. "I care about you."

He released her hand and dropped his arm to his side. His gaze moved over her then back to her eyes. "Nice jacket."

"It's yours."

"I know." He almost smiled but held back.

"You didn't answer me," she countered. "Are you okay? I didn't have a good reception on my phone. Moss's texts were brief. He said nobody was seriously hurt but your car got trashed."

"He was considerate not to worry you. But I gotta thank you. We almost didn't make it. Moss, Levi, and a medic, got to us just in time. Your text saved our lives," he told her. "Chamber and I were out burning off tension during the night when a twister caught us. We got rolled several times. When we regained consciousness, we realized we were pinned upside down inside my car. We weren't overly concerned until Chamber smelled gasoline. Everything gets murky from there. I slipped into that dark void. Next thing I knew, people were pulling us from the car. Moss said I freaked out on them, but they managed to get me out before the car exploded."

"Oh no . . . your beautiful car?"

He gave a short nod. "I can replace the car. I'm just thankful Chamber made it out alive. We were banged up quite a bit but in view of our dire situation, we got off easy."

Chamber walked over to them and offered Halo a bottled water. "Rebar tell you what happened?"

She accepted the water with a grateful smile. "Yes. It's terrifying. I was sitting in a motel that night praying. I couldn't shake the feeling that he was in danger."

A serious look flooded Chamber's piercing green eyes. "We figured it was the end of the road for us. And the last words I heard uttered from his lips before we blacked out were your names . . . *Cameo* and *Halo*."

Rebar shot him a disapproving look. "She doesn't need to know that."

"It was a dark night, Halo. I thank you for your prayers and the lifesaving message you sent to Moss." Chamber kissed her cheek then strolled back to the others.

"Rebar . . ." she practically breathed out his name and

looked at him through a haze of tears.

His focus shifted back to her. Their eyes met again.

"Will you let me hug you?" she asked.

He cocked one skeptical brow. "Won't your boyfriend get jealous?"

"Perhaps." She sighed. "But do you know how many times I thought of you during that road trip?"

"No. I wasn't there. You all took off without even telling the rest of us."

She saw the disappointment despite his outward stoicism. "It wasn't planned. We were seeking answers about Malika. She's been following me."

"The past week has been a hellish ordeal for me," he stated. "You haven't even wanted to so much as look at me for weeks. Now suddenly you're all caring and concerned? I sincerely appreciate your help and your prayers. But I'm over Malika, Camille, Shade, and all their bullshit."

"Fine." She slapped one hand on her hip. "Go ahead and act like a stubborn ass. Excuse me for caring." She swung away to leave.

His hand shot out and gripped hers. "Wait . . ."

She stopped but didn't turn around.

He reached for her other hand and pulled her about to face him. "I'm over them but I'll *never* be over you, babydoll."

The intensity in his voice, his eyes—was more than she could stand. She threw her arms around his neck in a fierce hug and buried her face in his hair. "I'm not over you either." She cried softly.

He wrapped both arms around her. His head dropped to the curve of her shoulder as they melded together in a tender embrace. She melted against him, breathing in his scent, relishing the feel of his silky hair against her cheek.

He slid one arm up the length of her back into her hair while keeping the other one around the small of her back. She felt him surrender to the pain, the longing, and the need for comfort. Everything about him felt familiar. The muscles of his chest, the way he held her as if she were a fragile doll, and mostly, the way he wrapped himself around her in the sweetest most affectionate manner like he needed her more than anything in the world.

He felt like home.

When they eased apart several timeless moments later, she touched his face. "I still have a lot to get through. When you're up for it, maybe we can talk, and you can tell me what the *other thing* was?"

Warmth returned to his eyes. "And maybe you can tell me about your impromptu road trip?"

"I'd like that very much," she replied. "I've missed our talks."

"So have I."

They unintentionally strolled away from the chatter on the patio across the lush uncut grass of Rush's huge yard.

"Are you going to be in Texas for a while?" she asked.

"If so, the only reason will be you. I've been thinking about going home."

She sighed. "I don't seem to have a home anymore. I miss my loft apartment." Thinking of her loft sparked a memory. She didn't want to ask but couldn't stop herself. "Have you taken anyone to your loft?"

"No. Everything is just as you left it. Your pillow, the little bottle of perfume you set on my dresser . . . your toothbrush. I couldn't bear to move any of it."

She was touched by the sentiment. Only true love held on like that.

"Perhaps it's time I get my own place again." She glanced back at Rush who was chatting with their friends. "The General's gone. It's just my mother who still needs help. Ricochet hasn't given up on her yet. There are important developments you need to know about."

"Hey, you two," Moss said in a welcoming tone as he approached. "Come join us for drinks and dinner on the patio. Shook said you have some shocking news."

Cameo nodded. "That's putting it mildly."

"Then come join the party. We have a lot to catch up on." He gave them an encouraging nod toward the patio.

She smiled agreeably. "We certainly do. We'll be right over.

Moss nodded and walked away.

Rebar balked. "I don't go down easy like Chamber did if your boyfriend decides to throw a punch over me hugging you."

She smiled in adoration. "Nobody's going to be hitting anyone. If I want to hug you, I will. Rush knew right from the start I wasn't over you and I never tried to pretend otherwise. I don't play games with people's hearts. He still wanted to risk it and date me."

"You're living with him. There's gotta be something serious between you."

"I don't know. We're taking it slow. With all that's been going on, I didn't have time to find my own place and he was rather persuasive with his invitation to stay with him. He's a good guy, Rebar."

Rebar arched one brow and scowled slightly. "Yep. Great guy. Made a move on my woman while I was out of my mind with worry."

"What?" She wandered farther away from the patio.

Rebar followed her. "In Santa Fe after the Raton disaster. Do you think I didn't know? I caught the subtle glances between you and Rush when we picked you up at the cantina. Then after I brought you home, you wouldn't leave your apartment." Rebar sighed disappointedly. "Baby, you had guilt painted all over your face."

Cameo gasped. "Why didn't you say anything?"

"Why didn't *you*?" He scoffed. "You could always tell me anything. You knew that. I figured there was only one reason you kept it secret and looked like I was right. Didn't take you long to move in with him."

"I . . . I can't believe you never mentioned it. Is that why you dumped me for Camille?"

"No. No way." Shame washed over his face. "I bear the guilt for that mess. Dumbest thing I've ever done. Just didn't have my head on straight."

She couldn't hide her disgrace and didn't try to. Tears stung her eyes over hurting him. "I'm glad this finally came out. It's been eating at me for weeks. Rush and I were in bad shape. He kissed me. Nothing else happened. Even so, I feel awful for being so weak."

"Did you kiss him back?"

She lowered her lashes. "Yes . . . I was desperate for any kind of comfort. But I'm not justifying what I did. I'm sorry I cheated on you."

"You didn't cheat on me," he said quietly. "Not for one minute do I believe he didn't know what he was doing. I would've understood how vulnerable you were. But when you refused to be open with me, I knew something had happened. Please give me a little credit and don't make him out to be some kind of hero. He's human just like the rest of us."

Her thoughts flashed back to what Rush had said during that trying time, *I like Rebar which is why he should never know. We could never be friends because I'm gonna take his woman.* The powerfully sensual way Rush stated his intent had lingered in her mind ever since. Then when Rebar broke up with her, she'd drifted to Texas in search of a fresh start.

Now here she was, torn up by emotion again.

"No. I knew his intent. He was quite clear on that. I shouldn't have given in to temptation," she said. "Then I tried to live behind a lie and that's on me. I'm equally to blame for the kiss. Rush didn't manipulate me. It just kinda happened. We were fighting for our lives and lost sight of everything else. Maybe I got what I deserved from Camille."

"Don't say that." He frowned. "What I did to you was way worse, unforgivable. I was insane to break up with you. I have no idea what was going on in my head that day. But it didn't last. Didn't take long to realize I made a huge mistake. You didn't deserve any of that. You were trying to help your mother, then you saved Rush's life, and he took advantage of the situation."

"Typical Damocles man." She sighed, while staring at his cross necklace.

"What?" Rebar tilted his head.

"Oh . . . um . . . dammit. I can't seem to keep anyone's secrets these days." She turned away but he caught her arm.

"Chamber told me that Rush has a necklace just like mine. I said, nah, just coincidence. What do you know?" Rebar asked.

She looked up at him slowly. "I can't carry anymore secrets. I can't do this anymore." She shifted her weight nervously. Tears brimmed and threatened to spill.

"What's going on?" He looked worried. "You can trust me with anything."

"You must swear to me that you'll tell nobody. Promise me." She knew if he gave his word, he'd stand by it.

"I swear, doll," he said in that tender way of his. "I'll not say a word. You look really upset. I'm getting nervous here."

Cameo drew a deep breath. "Tassos is Rush's father, too. Shade is the General's son, and Camille is pregnant," she blurted out in an airy rush, tears streaming down her cheeks. "Even worse, Malika and Shade are having an affair!"

He gripped her shoulders and stared down at her with blazing eyes. "What?"

"You heard me. Rush is your half-brother. You're not related to Shade at all, and your ex-girlfriend is pregnant."

"Pregnant to who?" Panicked drenched his voice. "Tell me it's not mine. Tell me I didn't ruin the rest of my life."

"It's Shade's baby . . . the General's grandson." She practically spat it out.

"Thank God," he said followed by a huge sigh. "How do you know all this?"

"Rush told me who his father was in Santa Fe, but he asked me to never tell anyone. He didn't want you or Shade to know."

"I can see why." Rebar scoffed. "He was after my girl."

Cameo half nodded. "I'm sorry."

"You're not to blame." Rebar looked toward the patio. Lines on his face tensed. "I'll keep your secret. How'd you find out about the rest? More deceit from Camille?"

"Malika. She followed me from state to state, leaving peculiar blue feathers and making uncanny appearances. It was disturbing. While I was out alone on a walk, she found me at a stream, and we talked a while. It felt like the sincerest conversation I've had with her. She's very afraid of Shade now."

"I don't believe that for a minute. Malika fears no one."

"Do you think she was telling the truth about Shade and Camille?"

"Possibly." Rebar was clearly running this new information through his brilliant mind. "Shade's paternity would explain his insane loyalty to that deviant. And I wouldn't put it past him to mess with Malika from what he said that day. But whatever game Malika's running now should be taken seriously. She's an expert at manipulation."

"She warned me that war is coming to Ricochet," Cameo added. "That Shade is furious."

"Yeah. I know Shade is pissed. He showed up at Moss's the night you left. That's why I was out blowing off steam in my car."

Her brows lifted. "Shade drove down to Texas? He tracked you down?"

"Yep. And I kicked his sorry ass."

She delicately touched a fading bruise just below his eye. "Is that the *other thing*?"

He gave a slight nod. "He's a bully. I'm not afraid of him. He made a few spineless threats. I told him come on back if he wanted another ass-kicking."

"Oh no. Do you think Malika was right about a war then?"

Rebar shrugged. "Doesn't matter. If he wants war, he'll get it. I'd rather live in peace, though. I've seen enough war. Either way, I'll never back down to Shade."

"I've always admired your silent strength. Very few people know you hold a Black Belt."

A slight smile touched his lips. "It's not something a true Black Belt brags about . . . as you would know. How many know about yours?"

"Very few." Her gaze swept his face, mentally trying to tend the injuries she saw. Sadness filled her over what he must've endured while she was away. "Are you okay, like, really okay? I can't believe you fought Shade and then got caught in a tornado. My gosh, Rebar . . ."

"I'm really okay." He smiled. "I'm not fragile."

"I'm sorry we left without telling you guys. Shook was worried about taking someone new to White Wolf's place."

"At least one member of this Ricochet family cares about me." He laughed a little, with heavy sarcasm in his voice.

"You were on my mind constantly," she admitted.

His expression softened. "For the record, Camille was never my girlfriend. Since we're finally being totally open with each other, you should know, it was just one night with her. I felt sullied afterward. All I could think about was you and how I hurt you. I didn't enjoy a single moment with her.

I mean that."

She searched his eyes for a hint of indecision and found none. "You really meant what you said to her in Amarillo?"

"Every word, and still do. My days of wavering ended after spending one night without you. I love you, baby. I never stopped. I won't stop even if you stay with Rush, I'll always love you. And I'm done trying to hide it."

"I wasn't supposed to tell anyone any of this," she said softly. "The only other one I told was Shook, only because Malika had targeted him. I felt he had a right to know. I think that's what they plan to meet about tonight. Shook will most likely fill them in. But nobody knows about Rush's paternity. You're the only one I told. I feel like such a fink."

He pulled her into a warm embrace. "No worries, doll. You've always been able to tell me anything. I'm the master of discretion, remember?"

She nodded against his chest and sniffed back tears.

"Hey," came Rush's voice, sounding agitated as he stalked toward them. "Don't ya think it's time the two of you join the party?" He walked straight up to them and looked at Cameo. "Why are you crying?" His gaze shifted between her and Rebar. "What did he say to upset you?"

She eased from Rebar's arms and looked up at Rush. "He didn't say anything." She burst into tears then took off running toward the house.

"Halo!" Rush called after her. "Wait!"

But she never slowed as she bolted into the kitchen, grabbed her bag and sprinted straight through the house, out the back door and down the path to his garage where freedom awaited.

Her car was parked just inside the first stall. She smacked her palm against the garage door opener, ducked under the door the moment it began to open and jumped behind the wheel of her Gran Sport.

By the time the garage door fully opened, she had the engine fired up and the car in gear. Rush and Rebar leapt out of the way as she barreled from the garage with her foot tromped on the gas.

She glanced in her rearview mirror on her way down the drive. Rebar didn't have a car. He must've ridden down with Chamber. However, Rush's Montego was not too far behind. Then she spotted Chamber's Hemi Cuda gaining on her as well. Rebar must've had the keys.

"Good luck, boys," she muttered while shifting gears. "Get ready to eat some Texas dust."

# CHAPTER THREE

R ush pushed his car hard, weaving through traffic while trying to keep his eyes on Cameo's gold GSX. She was flying. He wondered what had set her off. He knew she was still rebounding from his half-brother — a brother who did not yet know they shared the same father. He'd been watching them from a distance, giving Cameo space after their grueling road trip to South Dakota.

She'd been through an intense ordeal at White Wolf's cabin. He should've kept her closer to his side after they got back, but he hadn't considered Rebar a threat to his budding relationship with Cameo. As he mulled things over further, he recalled some of what she'd said during the excursion — missing her loft apartment, sitting on the window seat at night, Rebar's lodge, and his special Ramen dish he'd make for her.

*Maybe I underestimated probie.* Rush slammed his foot on the brake pedal to avoid hitting a car that ran a red light. He laid on the horn and cussed at the idiot. When he looked up, Cameo was nowhere in sight. That streaking flash of gold had vanished. He'd never be able to pinpoint her location in the bumper-to-bumper Dallas metro traffic, especially at night.

He pulled into the first parking lot and parked. Rebar followed him. They got out and eyeballed each other.

"I could've caught her in my car." Rebar sighed while gazing into the distance. "Had a 455 Stage One under the hood."

"Hey, this 428 Cobra Jet holds its own." Rush scowled.

"Wasn't fast enough to catch her now, was it?" Rebar shot

25

back. "And neither is this Hemi of Chamber's. Of course, had I not been bogged down in this Dallas traffic, maybe I could've caught her."

"None of that matters now. We lost her and she's headed to only God knows where." Rush sighed, scanning the horizon in hopes she'd turned around.

"She won't be back," Rebar said. "You don't know her very well, do ya?"

"Just as well as you do. You were with her what, a month or so?"

Rebar nodded. "Almost two months. But I took the time to get to know her. And one thing I've learned, if Cameo wants to get away, nothing can stop her."

"We can't just let her go. Any ideas, Einstein?"

Rebar rolled his eyes in obvious annoyance. "You come up with that term all on your own?" He scoffed. "We could run around like fools trying to find her. We could try her phone, but she won't answer in this state of mind. Or . . . we could round up the guys and cover key locations she might flee to."

Rush half frowned with a lowered brow. "You are a smart man. I'm surprised."

"I'm gonna take that as a compliment," Rebar said with an offhanded look. "Let's go back and devise a plan."

"The longer we take, the farther she'll go," Rush argued.

"She's gotta stop somewhere. She's only been in America since May, and only to a handful of states here in the Midwest. I suggest we narrow down the most likely locales and split up to search them." His focus shifted to the cross dangling from Rush's neck.

"What are you looking at?" Rush asked.

Rebar stared a few moments longer then replied, "Nothing."

They retreated to their vehicles and headed back to Rush's home. Rush led the way. While driving, he pondered Rebar's confidence and how quickly the man's mind worked. He also thought about the way Rebar had noticed his necklace. He'd noticed Rebar's, too. They appeared identical, furthering Cameo's claim that Tassos had fathered them both. Even if they shared the same father, at least Shade was no longer part of the equation. Rush felt he might be able to acknowledge Rebar's kinship one day, depending on how things went.

He wondered if Cameo had caved and told Rebar they were half-brothers.

*Nah. She wouldn't.* He assumed she told him the shocking news Malika had dropped while up in Pine Ridge. He couldn't think of any other reason she'd be upset. And on that thought, he realized they needed to update the members of Ricochet before taking off in search of Cameo.

"Did you find her?" Shook asked the minute Rush stepped from his car.

"No. She was making tracks." Rush shook his head. "Damn. That car of hers can move."

Shook's brows furrowed. "Why'd she run off?"

"I don't know." Rush caught Rebar's subtle glare. "She just needs to blow off tension. She'll be back when she cools down."

"Hey, Rebar. How ya doing?" Shook asked. "I heard you had a close call with Mother Nature."

Rebar laughed a little. "Yeah. She rolled us a few times."

They walked together back to the patio a few feet behind Rush. He listened to them make small talk and admired Shook for doing a better job than him of making Rebar feel welcome.

*My own brother and I couldn't even get past my jealousy to ask how he was feeling.* Rush sighed. He almost liked Rebar, but their mutual love for Cameo posed a problem.

"Where's Halo?" Moss asked as the three men straggled back to the gathering.

"Seems she needed a breather," Rush told them. "She's a

smart woman. I'm sure she just needed to reconnect with that fast car of hers."

"That's how Rebar and I got rolled by the twister," Chamber said. "What's the weather forecast tonight?"

Everyone pulled out their phone.

"Dammit," Rush growled. "Storm's moving in."

Levi cocked a look. "What do you expect, mate? It's mid-August." He turned toward Rebar. "Can you track her?"

"No," Rebar replied. "Today's the first time I've seen her in a while. My devices are good, but I need access to the host to initiate tracking."

"We need to split up and launch a search," Rush told them. "We can't just leave her wandering around out there in tornado alley."

The guys nodded in agreement.

"Before we split up again, can you give us a quick rundown on what happened at Pine Ridge?" Moss asked. "Shook said y'all had shocking news."

Rush nodded. "Probably be best if he tells you. He knows more than the rest of us."

Everyone looked expectantly at Shook.

"Can it wait?" he asked. "Shouldn't we find Halo first?"

"That may take all night," Rush said. "The guys deserve an update, like Moss said, before we go back on the road."

Shook hesitated but relented, looking somewhat troubled. "Malika was making mysterious appearances to Halo then vanishing in a puff of blue smoke," he began. "Everyone here but Rebar knows I was raised by a Lakota Medicine Man. We decided to seek his wisdom on the matter, since Malika is also Lakota. What we encountered we'll never forget. And I found out the truth about something I always suspected, White Wolf is my natural father."

"Whoa, that's incredible," Levi said. "I bet you were happy."

"Yeah," Shook agreed. "Spending time with him as father and son was pretty cool." He briefed them on the two dances and how Malika tried to pull Cameo away. Then he filled them in on what Cameo had told him regarding Malika, Shade, and Camille. "But there's something I withheld back up there, even from Stoke, Rider and Rush," he added with an apologetic glance at Rush. "Sorry, buddy, but Halo was already consumed with guilt over breaking her mother's confidence with me. We decided it would be best to drop this bombshell when the whole family was together."

"What could be worse than Malika and Shade having an affair while Camille's carrying his child?" Moss asked, eyes wide.

Shook took a heavy breath and exhaled. "Remember how nobody could grasp Shade's loyalty to a man that nobody's ever seen? And how Shade's troop just did as commanded, no questions asked then money was dropped into their accounts?"

A flurry of nods traveled around the group.

"That's how it was," Rebar said. "Jackson would tell us a message came in from the General. We'd go on assignment and an automatic deposit came in when we were done."

"Yep," Chamber agreed. "We never bothered to question it. Not sure why."

"Well, we now know why Shade was fiercely loyal to a human trafficking tyrant," Shook told them. "The General was Shade's biological father. Shade bears no relation whatsoever to Rebar. Nadia and the General had a son, the General's one and only offspring, before the man's war accident left him sterile."

"Whoa." Rush felt the wind knocked out of him. *Why hadn't Cameo confided in me before going to Shook with such life-changing information?* "Halo told you this?"

"She did," Shook replied. "We agreed to keep it under wraps until we got back. She's worried for her mother's safety if Shade finds out Malika unveiled his darkest secret."

"I can't believe Halo didn't tell me," Rush muttered.

"Hey, don't go there," Shook said. "She didn't even wanna tell me. I found her sitting alone looking tense. My father had been needling her conscience. The lady was a nervous wreck. I promised her we'd wait until we got back to disclose this part. With all we went through up there, adding this would've been way too much. We felt something of this magnitude should be shared with the entire family together."

"I just wish she was here to tell us about her experience with Malika," Rider said.

"Me, too." Stoke sighed. "That girl has had way too much to deal with lately."

"We'd like to hear more about Halo's run-in with Malika," Levi said.

Shook's gaze swept the gathering. "Later. Anyone think we should check on Halo now?"

Rush decided they'd talked enough. "We can get into that another time. Malika is a complicated woman. Shook's right, we gotta fan out and find Halo before severe weather does. She doesn't know her way around very well yet."

"You got a plan?" Shook asked.

"Yeah. Actually, it was probie's idea." Rush glanced at Rebar then back to the others. "We split up and search places she might go to."

"Maybe she went back to Denver," Chamber said.

Rush shrugged. "She did mention missing home. But she also might figure that's the first place we'll look. And I doubt she'd wanna be anywhere near Camille or Shade right now."

"How about Amarillo?" Shook asked. "She's been there."

"Or Raton?" Moss suggested. "If she's flashing back, she may remember it as a good place to blend."

"What about Austin? She has a good memory with Rush there," Shook pointed out.

"We also have some history in Santa Fe during our escape from the General after I got shot," Rush said. "She actually returned to Larita's Bar to get my necklace back." He caught Rebar's shift in disposition. His half-brother seemed to bristle at the mention of Santa Fe.

Rebar pushed to his feet. "Chamber and I will ride up to Denver and search the area just in case. I know that area better than anyone here. I'd kinda like to check in at my lodge anyway."

"Good idea." Rush gave him a nod then looked around the group. "Levi, Moss, how about staying in Dallas in the event she returns home. She's got a key to my house so maybe pop in frequently to see if she returned."

"Sounds good to us," Moss agreed. "We'll crash at my place when not out searching."

"Rider, Stoke . . . can you guys cover the roads between here and Raton? Amarillo is right along the way. I seriously doubt she'd return to Amarillo but I'm not ruling out Raton from what Moss said. Our bond began in Raton."

"Yeah sure," Stoke said with a short laugh. "We've got nothing better to do than take an eight-hour ride through tornado alley during a storm."

Rider grinned. "Ah don't be such a sissy."

"I was being sarcastic," Stoke retorted. "Did you not hear the humor in my voice?" He gave Rider a playful shove.

"We best hit the road then," Rider said. "We've got a lot of ground to cover. If she's on that route, we'll find her."

"I hear that." Rush stated. "Shook and I will ride with you guys up through Amarillo then keep going onto Santa Fe. With eight of us scouring the highways, we'll find her."

"Are we done?" asked Chamber. "Times a wastin'."

Rush cast him a disciplinary glance. "Never a waste of time to devise a well-thought plan before embarking on a mission. I want you all to check every Truckstop, food mart, and well-

lit gas station along the way. Ask clerks if they've seen her."
He made one final glance around his group. "Everyone on the
same page here?"

"Yep." Rebar nodded.

The others responded in the same manner.

"Let's move out then. Keep your phones on and text me
with any leads so we can stay organized," he told them.

After all the riders had taken leave, Rush secured the house
then found Shook in the garage. "You wanna travel by car or
bike?"

"I'm not afraid of a little rain. We'll have better visual on
bikes and get around faster," Shook replied while inspecting
his Harley.

"Sounds good to me. Rider and Stoke already took off.
Maybe we should head straight to Santa Fe."

"You have a feeling she's headed there?"

Rush shrugged then straddled the leather seat of his bike.
"She braved going to Larita's by herself just to bargain for my
necklace. That little cantina holds memories for us, and the
people there welcomed her. Seems she made inroads with the
owner because of her generosity."

"Halo has that effect on everyone." Shook smiled. "Even
my old-fashioned father adored her. White Wolf doesn't
warm to strangers easily. But he did to her."

"Yeah . . ." Rush paused before starting the engine. "Like
father like son, huh?"

"If you've got a point to make, just say what's on your
mind, man."

Typical Shook, straightforward and confident.

"I saw you kiss her. The two of you looked a little too cozy
at White Wolf's cabin. The way you danced, the whole Lakota
connection thing."

Shook didn't say anything right away. He mounted his
bike and keyed the ignition. "I won't deny that I felt close to

her up there, or that I enjoyed the connection. The thing about stealing someone's gal, Rush, is she may never be all yours. Halo is still very much a free spirit. You got her to move in with you on the rebound, but that lady is nowhere near ready for a serious commitment."

"You always have been direct." Rush felt a little karma coming his way. He pushed the foreboding feeling aside. "I can offer her something neither you nor Rebar can . . . a fresh start. I haven't slept with her mother or sister."

"Touché." Shook laughed. "Be careful about getting too cocky, though, my friend. You know what they say about love and war."

Rush slanted a delving look his way before they fired up the bikes and headed out. Until now, he'd felt confident that Halo was his and only his. She'd promised not to date anyone else while they were together. He couldn't consider Shook's kiss a move on her part. Clearly, they hadn't known he was watching from a distance.

*Did Shook think I'd not keep an eye on my woman?*

He was taken back by his friend's blatant response. Rush wasn't about to make a scene over their secret little powwow and the kiss. But he couldn't erase it from his mind.

The Lakota ties that Shook shared with Cameo seemed powerful and Rush had to admit to himself that he felt more threatened by that than her past with Rebar.

In addition to that, there was the dance. The way Shook and Cameo had danced around the fire in a ritualistic manner was unmistakably sensual. Though the dance was performed solely to lure Malika out, Rush couldn't help but feel jealous. He'd danced with Cameo. He knew the intense sensuality she emanated when dancing. She was indeed a wild thing.

At this point, Rush wondered if Shook posed a bigger threat than Rebar. He genuinely believed Cameo was over Rebar. Even so, his jealousy had reared when he saw them hugging. He was relieved Rebar wanted to head back to Denver.

Rush knew Cameo would never seek solace in a place that carried sadness and the threat of crossing paths with Camille and Shade.

*At least the probie is out of the way for now.*

He settled into pace beside Shook. They sped northwest toward Santa Fe. He visually scanned every car they passed, every Truckstop and food mart. Her rare car would stand out like a beacon if they crossed paths or spotted it.

He didn't want to risk missing her.

She was out there somewhere and with thunderheads rolling in, she had most likely pulled over to shelter until the threatening storm passed, unless PTSD had flung her into that dark place where she became disoriented. In that case, she might ignore the weather and push straight through to a place that felt familiar.

And the place she'd likely seek out would be where they had shared their first tender moments and felt the chemistry.

Either way, he felt confident that he and Shook were on the right course.

# CHAPTER FOUR

After riding hard all night, Rush and Shook rolled into Santa Fe shortly after dawn, ten hours after leaving Dallas. He ignored the road fatigue and focused on Cameo. They pulled into Larita's even though Cameo's Gran Sport was nowhere in sight. Rush had sent a group text to the others, hoping one of them had seen her but maybe their texts hadn't come through.

"Any word?" Shook asked from his parked bike. He chugged a bottled water.

"Not yet." Rush angled one hand over his brow and scanned the area for any sign of Cameo's car in the event she'd parked away from the cantina. *Nothing.*

"Let's go in and ask around," Shook suggested. "Maybe get a bite to eat."

"Yeah." Rush agreed, feeling a little defeated.

They sauntered into the bar. A lovely Hispanic girl was serving the breakfast crowd. She looked up and smiled when she saw him. Rush gave her a polite nod He remembered her from before. He and Shook found a table and took a seat.

She approached with menus. "Hola, my friends. You look well."

"Larita, your English sounds great. Have you been taking lessons?" Rush asked the petite raven-haired beauty.

"Sí sí, señor. My husband teach me."

"You are married now?"

She flashed a stunning diamond ring. "Ah, sí, sí. You like ring?"

Rush nodded. "Almost as lovely as you."

" You like eat?" she asked.

"The breakfast special," he replied. "Everything you cook is delicious."

She thought for a moment, obviously translating his words in her mind then she nodded. "I bring nice special this day. You not here much."

"¿Te acuerdas de la hermosa dama con la que estaba?"

"What did you say?" Shook asked.

"I asked if she remembered the beautiful lady I was with."

"Sí."

"Has she been here?" Rush hoped Larita understood shorter sentences.

"No. Not since she give ring. I sorry." Then her head shot up and she smiled. "There is lady now, señor." She pointed toward the counter.

Rush's spirit soared when he saw Cameo sitting at the counter. She wasn't wearing the same clothes that she'd left in, but he knew she always kept an emergency backpack in her car. She appeared to have ditched her riding leathers for faded jeans, a slinky black top and sexy ankle boots.

Shook swung around in the booth. "I'll be damned. You were right to come here. Maybe you do have the strongest bond with her after all."

Rush didn't even try to hide his proud grin. "Wait here. I wanna speak with her first, make sure she's okay."

"No argument here. I'm hungry. I'll wait on the food."

Rush swaggered across the small, crowded room, feeling damn pleased with himself. His intuition had been spot-on. The probie would be in Denver soon, giving Rush plenty of time to take Cameo home and calm her down, get her intimately settled in away from outside influence.

"Hey, angel," he said softly upon his approach. He laid a hand on the back of her waist-length blonde hair.

She flinched at his touch and spun toward him on her stool. "Oh . . . you," she muttered. "Just what I need. More trouble."

"You're not in trouble, babe. "We've all been crazy with worry and everyone's searching for you. Are you okay?"

Her brows knitted together over those sultry blue eyes in a quizzical expression. "You think I'm Cameo?"

"That is your name. But the guys call you *Halo*. Did you black out last night? You must've driven all night to get here before us."

"Um . . . I did drive all night. But I'm not Cameo. And I really don't need hassles. I've had a horrible night."

He studied her closely, baffled by her confusion. He suspected she'd regressed into a PTSD episode again. "Rebar must've really done a number on you again, didn't he, babe?"

"Ha! Rebar! You're joking!. Last time I saw him was in Amarillo and he made his feelings about me crystal clear."

"Okay . . . we're not making progress here. Now, try to relax and focus. We're dating and you're living with me. I figured you'd come here because of my necklace and our memories of this place," he told her quietly, calmly.

Her focus went to his pendant. She stared at it for a few minutes as if thinking, then exclaimed, "Ohhh . . . you're my sister's guy, the one with the cross necklace. Rush, is it? She pointed you out in Amarillo after you led us from the house. Thanks, by the way. Cameo is lucky to have such a great group of guys."

*Not possible!* He thought. No way could Camille be sitting here right now while Ricochet was hunting for her twin. *No way is a coincidence like this possible. Unless . . .* His thoughts rambled.

"If you're Camille, then what have you done with your sister? Did Malika catch up to her? Is this a trick?" His jaw clenched.

"Don't even mention Malika to me right now," she hissed. "I drove all night to try and forget what I saw."

Rush was utterly mystified. "Would you like to join me and Shook for breakfast?" He nodded toward their table, hoping food and rest would bring her around.

"The FBI guy?"

"That's him."

"Wow. He looks different without all the makeup."

He wrinkled his brows, perplexed by how genuine she sounded. "C'mon, babe. Maybe after some food your mind will clear."

She shrugged and hopped off the stool. He led her to the table. The moment she slid into the booth, Shook visibly bristled.

"What's *she* doing here?" he asked.

Rush scowled. "What's wrong with you, man? Is that any way to greet my angel?"

"This one an angel?" He laughed sardonically. "Hardly. This is Cameo's twin. Is she messing with your head?"

"I tried to tell him," she sassed. "I'm not Cameo. I'm the twin."

"You're serious?" Rush stared hard in disbelief. She looked like Cameo's clone. He wondered if his road lag was clouding his senses. She looked and sounded every bit like his woman.

"Look, fellas. I know how you feel about me. Sorry I'm not the angelic twin you're looking for. Why *are* you looking for her anyway?" Camille snapped.

"Something happened last night that set her off. She bolted and we can't find her." Rush shifted his attention to Shook. "How'd you know this wasn't Cameo?"

"You wouldn't understand." Shook tossed money on the table and slid from the booth. "I'll be outside. I can't sit here with her."

A dejected expression crossed Camille's face. Rush felt bad, but for the life of him didn't understand why he felt anything toward her. He was still trying to grasp how Cameo's twin ended up at Larita's Bar.

"If you don't believe me, just look outside. My white Shelby is parked in front," she told him.

He leaned toward the window. Sure enough, a sharp white Shelby Mustang GT sat shining beneath the morning sun.

"Why are you here? What have you done with Cameo?" he demanded.

"I didn't do anything with Cameo. And I really don't know why I stopped here. Maybe because it's where we picked you and Cameo up when you got shot. Do you recall me trying to examine your bullet wound that day?"

"Somewhat. Wasn't one of my better days."

Sympathy fluttered through her eyes. "I'm glad you recovered."

"Thanks." He took a drink of water. "Why are you here?"

"Not sure I should tell you by the reaction of your buddy."

Rush sighed. "He's cool. Just shocked. Are you gonna tell me or not? I've got better things to do than play games."

Sadness washed over her face. "I'm done with my mother's manipulations. Believe it or not, I came here to ask if anyone knew how to find you. I have nowhere else to go."

"What do you mean? You're engaged to Shade." Rush didn't ignore his suspicion that this could be a Malika ploy.

"I walked in on my mother and Shade yesterday. Things got heated before I emptied his gun, then I threw my ring at him and took off."

His eyes widened. "Did you kill them? Is that why you're on the run?

"Of course not," she huffed. "I'm not Cameo. I don't just shoot people in the heat of a moment. I put the scare of the devil into them, though, before I left."

"Are you sure that was wise? You're carrying his child."

"What? Who told you that?" she snapped.

"Malika followed us to South Dakota. You should know, you drove her."

Camille appeared even more surprised. "What? I've never been to South Dakota. And I'm definitely *not* pregnant." She stood and pulled her shirt up. "Do I look pregnant to you?"

He stared at her perfectly flat and quite lovely stomach. She certainly wasn't shy. He caught a glimpse of her bare breasts. For a woman rumored to be three months along, she sure hid it well.

"No . . . you look very nice, actually. But I can't trust you. You worked with Malika before, this we know. Do you deny it?"

She sat back down and hung her head. "No. I don't deny it. What I did was horrible, hurting my sister that way. She said she forgave me but it's a lot to forgive. Shade wants revenge on Rebar for betraying the troop, so he set me up to find Rebar's tracking device. He told me to seduce him if I had to. But yesterday . . ." She released a quivering sigh. "Yesterday I heard the whole disgusting truth about what Shade and Malika are doing." Tears glistened in her eyes. "I'm certain Malika will try to find me. But Shade is trying to get rid of me. I don't know what to do. So I came here as a last resort, hoping to find out where you guys hang out so I could ask for help. If I could just talk to my sister, I know she'd understand."

He weighed her words carefully while observing her facial expressions and body language. Everything he'd heard should've compelled him to walk away right then and never look back. However, what he saw made him stay. She appeared genuinely distraught. Ricochet's purpose was to help women and children out of bad situations. If this woman was telling the truth and he denied her help, he'd bear the guilt if anything happened to her.

On the other hand, Camille could be a mole sent in by

Malika and Shade to do more damage to his increasingly fragile relationship with Cameo and cause more dissention within Ricochet's ranks. He knew that most, or all the guys, would object to helping this one. The burden was on his shoulders alone at what to do.

Would helping Camille drive Cameo farther away? Or could it possibly further their relationship and bring his lady much needed peace?

He waved Larita over. "Breakfast for the lady, please."

She nodded politely and hurried away.

Rush leaned back and casually stretched both arms across the back of the booth. "Convince me why I should take a huge risk and help you? You've never been the damsel in distress from what I know about you."

"I've done some bad things. Helped Missy and Joan abduct Shade. Destroyed what my sister had with Rebar and tried to steal from him. I haven't been nice to Cameo either. She's tried a few times to make peace with me, but I was a bitch about it. I guess I was jealous, not that she had Rebar, but of their loving relationship. I've been miserably unhappy with Shade for the past six months and didn't know why. He just wasn't interested in me anymore. He didn't care what I did or how many hours I put into working in the garage."

"You work in a garage?" Rush was surprised. He glanced at her fingernails and sure enough, there was a little dirt under them. "Guess I should've looked at your hands first. I see now that you are not Cameo."

"No, that's for sure. She's refined. I restore cars. I've always had a passion for them, and I love to fix things. Shade wanted me to get my doctorate. I thought that would please him. I remember how disappointed he was when I quit nursing. So I started taking classes."

Rush tried to stay on track throughout the choppy conversation, though he longed to hear more about her restoration work. "Shade was ignoring you?"

She nodded. "I'm speculating that he lost interest in me when he found Malika."

"Bear with me as I try to wrap my mind around this. You didn't drive Malika to South Dakota, you're not pregnant, and Shade is carrying on with your mother. Is that your tale?"

"Not a tale." She frowned. "The truth. I know nothing about South Dakota or why my mother was there."

"You're absolutely certain they're having an affair?"

"Oh . . . I'm sure about that all right. They didn't know my class got canceled. I saw Malika walk past the garage, then I saw them kissing on the porch." She grimaced in disgust. "Not just a friendly kiss either. They never saw me sneak into the house then up the stairs. I sat outside the bedroom door and listened to every sordid detail of their appalling schemes, from Shade's abduction to what they're plotting now."

His interest piqued. "Does it involve my family?"

She nodded. "They want revenge. Shade has it out for Rebar, and Malika said Shook's in *her* crosshairs. They discussed using me and Cameo as pawns in some crazy war against Ricochet." She dropped her head in her hands as if exhausted from mental overload.

"Would you be willing to tell us everything you know?" He still felt apprehensive about her presence. The timing felt eerie. Nevertheless, if she had inside info on Shade and Malika, taking her in might be worth the risk.

Her eyes met his. "I'll tell you everything I know and help you stop them, in exchange for protection. Malika is trying to gain Cameo's trust. But if she can't, if my sister and I don't go along with their vendetta against your group, then she's going to crush us, too."

"She said that?"

"Yes . . . to Shade."

"I'd like to take you back to one of our homes. We can stash your car in a garage once we check it for tracking devices."

"You think this is a trick?" A pained look swept over her face.

"I have a family to protect. We do this my way or no way. I've already got my work cut out getting the rest of the guys to accept this. Hopefully, if you're seriously being truthful, they'll agree to help."

"What if they don't?"

He reached over and held her hand. "We'll cross that bridge if we come to it. My guys are cool. I want to hear their thoughts after you meet with them."

"Thank you." She squeezed his fingers with her dainty hand. "Thank you for giving me a chance."

He gave her a nod and withdrew his hand. "Better eat your food. We've got a long drive ahead of us. After I get you to safety, I gotta resume the search for Cameo. You're gonna have to hang with a couple of the guys in the meantime. Can you do that without a fuss?"

"Yes. Anything to get away from Shade. I won't cause you trouble."

He laughed a little. "Famous last words."

Rush realized this woman was highly skilled in manipulation and far above average intelligence. But he wasn't Rebar. He didn't have a history with her or unresolved feelings. Rebar had been a sitting duck when this female worked him over. Rush made a mental note to never forget what Cameo's twin was capable of.

Even so, she captivated him. He wanted to chat further with her about what she knew, her restoration business and passion for cars. From what he'd heard, she was quite a survivalist, too. He wondered if she'd share the infamous story of the Louisiana abduction.

Chamber had told them his side. However, Rush imagined hearing the tale straight from Camille herself would be fascinating and lend insight to her motives. He also wondered how much she knew about Shade and the General. Taking her in could prove beneficial to Ricochet.

Knowledge was power, and Rush always tried to keep up with who was doing what out there, especially because of their type of work.

"Malika told your sister something about Shade that is quite shocking. I wonder if you can confirm it?"

She looked up from her plate. "What could be more shocking than him screwing my mother?"

"Something about his father. Did you hear anything along those lines?" He wanted to test her willingness to disclose information.

"Oh, that. Shade's father was the General. It's true. I heard him and Malika discussing it. I confronted him during my outburst. He said the General was a private man and he couldn't break his trust. I'm still trying to process everything. I went ballistic."

"I'm sorry he hurt you." Rush sat back again and let her eat in peace.

After Camille finished eating, Rush threw some money on the table with what Shook had left there, enough to cover three breakfasts instead of two, and ushered her outside. Shook sat waiting on his parked bike, not a happy camper.

"We're gonna take her back to Moss's place. We'll comb her car for tracking then hide it in my garage," Rush told him. "She's willing to share everything she knows in exchange for protection. I think her information will shine a light on all the shadows we've been dealing with."

Shook cocked a cynical brow then held up his cellphone. "Cameo messaged me."

Rush glanced at Camille to make sure she wasn't trying to sneak a peek then he read the text.

*Shook, this is Halo.*

*I'm safe so tell Rush to stop chasing me.*

*I need time alone to think.*
*I'll be in touch when I'm ready.*
"Did you track it?"
"Can't track a text. Sorry, mate."

Rush walked to his bike, head down. He struggled to hide the nagging jealousy in his gut. Cameo had taken off and texted his best friend instead of him. Ever since Malika's first appearance as *Feather Blue*, Cameo had gradually withdrawn into herself.

And she seemed to be pulling away from him.

First by hiding the feather he knew she carried but hadn't yet told him about. Then wearing Rebar's jacket instead of her own. And not telling him about Malika's second visitation after the tornado but had privately texted Moss and asked him to check on Rebar. At White Wolf's cabin, she seemed closer to Shook than anyone. And now this. She'd been gone for twelve hours and chose Shook as the one to message.

He sensed her drifting but didn't know how to reel her back in. He knew his lifestyle differed vastly from what she was used to. She abhorred hunters, didn't care for fishing, and wasn't fond of hanging around the nightly campfires. Despite her background in Forestry and Wildlife Preservation, she preferred spending her free time indoors.

He began to realize they had little in common. Even so, he believed their mutual attraction was strong enough to bridge those gaps.

They did share a passion for muscle cars, and he found her independent spirit irresistible. All the guys adored her. And she was graciously humble in return. She respected the boundaries and never gave him cause to doubt her integrity.

Even the kiss between her and Shook had appeared one-sided. Rush couldn't very well go off on his best friend about one short kiss at White Wolf's cabin. Emotions had run high among the men during that experience. Forbearance in unique situations was required on his part as leader.

However, this felt different. His girl had bolted, after hugging Rebar no less. *Then she texted Shook to tell me to back off.* He wasn't sure how to handle this. Once they got Camille settled, Rush was determined to find Cameo whether she liked it or not. One text message telling him to stop looking was not enough to deter him.

He straddled the seat of his Harley and looked over at Camille standing between him and Shook. "Let's hit the road. Once we get this one settled in, I'm going back out in search of Halo," he told Shook then turned his attention to Camille. "Keep that Shelby of yours between us. One wrong move and you'll be fodder for Shade and Malika to scrape off the road, got it?"

She nodded, then slid behind the wheel of her car. He'd never met identical twins — it felt bizarre yet enthralling. Even her voice sounded like Cameo's.

"What about the text?" Shook asked. "You're not gonna respect Halo's request?"

"I'm not letting one short message stop me from finding her. We can't even be sure she sent the message. Malika and Shade may be holding her captive and sending the text. Until I'm certain that message is from Halo, I won't stop searching."

"Have you tried calling her?"

"All night," Rush replied with a sigh. "No answer."

Shook pulled up beside him and leaned in close. "Hey, I gotta tell you something. After I got the text, I tried Halo's number while you were inside with Camille. I didn't wanna say anything in front of *her*."

An ominous chill raced up Rush's arms. "Tell me Shade and Malika don't have Halo."

"It didn't sound like it. She said she was alone but wouldn't tell me where she was."

"You spoke to her? She took your call?" He felt the ground drop out from under him.

"Just briefly. She didn't wanna talk."

"Where the hell is she then?"

"The call came in from Austin. Maybe she went back to that hotel the two of you stayed at," Shook replied.

Rush couldn't believe how far off-course he'd been. "She was only a couple hours away and we wasted all this time going in the opposite direction?"

"Smart woman. She probably checked the weather and hid out there for the night. It's anyone's guess where she'll go now."

"You mentioned Austin, didn't you?"

"Yep."

"And I never even considered it. Do you have a supernatural connection to her?" Rush asked, frustrated.

"Not that I'm aware of. Just figured since she has happy memories there . . . but you had your mind set on Santa Fe. I didn't wanna argue."

Rush shook his head, angry with himself for ignoring his friend's intuition. His jealousy had cost them precious time.

He glanced at Camille sitting in her car, waiting. *Maybe there is a valid reason I felt so strongly about driving ten hours to this little cantina.*

Crossing paths with Camille bordered on supernatural. No way could Shade or Malika have known his destination point, or what time he'd arrive in this dusty town. The only people who knew Ricochet's itinerary were the eight members. And not one of them were allies with the General's son and his mistress.

*No. This is fate.* He started his engine. "The plan stays the same. After we get the twin to safety, I'm going back out to find Halo and bring her home."

Disapproval furrowed Shook's brow. "Just so you know, I'm not okay with this. That woman is trouble. You've lost your mind to take Shade's pregnant fiancée back to Ricochet."

"She's not pregnant. Just another Malika lie. And she's no

longer Shade's anything. Camille was quite clear on the facts. Malika's trying to start a war."

"I'm still not onboard with taking her in." Anger resounded in Shook's voice as he prepared to ride.

"There are eight of us and one of her. We'll be fine," he refuted Shook's warning.

Rush sent a quick group text rallying all the guys back to Dallas. He didn't want to waste their time and energy, or keep the family split up longer than necessary. Since Cameo had hunkered down close to homebase, he figured she wouldn't go far. She simply needed time to sort whatever had upset her.

The sensible thing was for the guys to hang around the area and keep an eye out for her while Rush went off on his own to do some extensive searching. He didn't get a sense that Shade had her. Though Shade's drilling company was based in Houston, the man no longer lived in Texas. Rumor among riggers was that Shade hadn't been seen in Texas since he'd moved to Colorado Springs with Camille.

Malika, on the other hand, was a mystery. She had the inexplicable ability to appear anywhere and vanish with a puff of smoke. Rush did worry that Cameo's mother might find her before he did. And that was why he refused to let scanty information stop him.

However, Ricochet had cargo now. They needed to hear more of what Camille knew, get her tucked in and comb every inch of her car for anything suspicious before hiding it in his garage. And as leader of the family, he couldn't resume his search until this immediate problem was addressed.

Two women, identical twins, yet both in dangerous situations. Rush contemplated everything backward and forward the entire ride back to Dallas. What he feared most was losing Halo over offering refuge to her twin. Nevertheless, Ricochet had always placed their purpose ahead of personal feelings.

For the first time since he'd started this group and became their leader, Rush questioned his ability to do just that. *How can I focus on helping this woman when my heart is out there somewhere?*

# CHAPTER FIVE

Rush pulled into Moss's driveway, followed by Camille and Shook, turned off his bike, and dismounted. He took off his helmet and looked at Moss who had come out of the door to greet them.

"You found her!" Moss rushed up to them. "Wait . . . that's not Halo's car," he recanted.

"No . . ." Rush sighed. "Who we found was Halo's twin. I have no idea how she ended up at the cantina the exact same time we did. I'm exhausted. But we need the car searched thoroughly. You know what to do."

Shook had parked behind Camille after she pulled into the driveway. "Behave yourself," he warned her then walked to the house.

"Whoa, he seems pissed," Moss noted.

"I think this is a bit more personal for him because of his undercover stint with Malika."

"No," Shook hollered from the door. "That has nothing to do with it. Camille's a vindictive bitch, it's that simple."

"Okay . . ." Moss exhaled and shrugged. "No tension here."

"What's the status on everyone else?" Rush asked, keeping his eyes on Camille as she stood close to her car.

"Rider and Stoke should be here shortly. Levi's inside. No word from Chamber or the probie yet."

"How about giving them a call," Rush suggested. "Just in case probie was right about Halo."

Moss pulled out his phone and tapped the keypad. "Hey,

mate. Rush and Shook just got back. What's up with you guys?" He tapped speaker so Rush could listen.

"No sign of her," Chamber replied. "We arrived in Denver this morning. Drove past her old apartment, asked around everywhere. Nobody's seen her. Rebar knows a lot of peeps up here, restaurant owners and so forth. We'll go back out in the morning and keep looking."

"Didn't you get the group message to rally back here?" Rush asked, agitated.

"Uh, no, mate. Nothing." Chamber replied. "Did you forget to add us?"

Rush looked at his phone. "Shit. Sorry, man. My mind was tripping after we ran into Halo's twin. What are the chances of that happening?"

"You did what?" Chamber asked.

"Shook and I searched all night from here to Santa Fe. We were at Larita's when Camille walked in. I thought it was Halo. There's been an unusual turn of events. I want everyone to hear what this chick has to say."

"Looks like we're gonna have to listen in on a video call," Chamber said. "Kinda wiped out from the drive up and searching all day."

"I hear ya," Rush agreed. "We've been on the road nonstop since last night. We gotta get this new one settled in, and her car scanned before a meeting. How about we call you and probie in the morning?"

"That'll work," Chamber said. "We were getting ready to turn in for the night."

"Can't believe I forgot to add them to the text." Rush handed Moss his phone. "I must be too tired. Let's get Camille to your guest room. She should be safe here."

A wary expression flashed across Moss's face. "Are you sure? Shade was here."

"Say what? When?" Rush rubbed his tired eyes.

"Never got a chance to tell you. While you were up in South Dakota, Shade made a surprise appearance. He wanted answers from Rebar. Probie kicked his ass. Levi and I pulled in after work just as the fight was under way. Blood all over my yard."

"Whose blood?"

"Mostly Shade's. Fortunately, just the grass." Moss laughed. "Rebar's tough, man. No love lost there. Then again, they were never related. Geez. I can't keep up these days."

"I know the feeling." Rush sighed. "Can't believe Shade had the gall to show his face here. How'd he even find out that Rebar was here?"

"Nobody knows. But he did say he'd be back. Maybe you should take the woman elsewhere. If she's on the run from him, this isn't the safest place for his fiancée."

"Ex-fiancée now," Rush clarified. "She caught him in bed with Malika."

"It's true then."

"Seems so."

Moss shook his head. "You best take her out of here. back to your place. I don't want Shade showing up here causing more trouble. Why'd you bring her back with you anyway?"

"She asked me to. She's afraid and hurting and currently homeless," Rush replied.

"And trouble," Moss added. "Look, Levi and I will scan the car and bring it over later tonight. You take *Little Miss Intent* back to your place. You have more rooms and are better secluded, plus Stoke and Rider are hanging with ya. I have a feeling Shook is staying here for the night."

Rush nodded halfheartedly. He didn't relish the idea of Camille bunking at his place. However, Moss made valid points. This would be the first place Shade would look for Camille. Without knowing all the facts, he had to protect his friends.

"All right. I'll take the girl with me. Bring the car over when it's cleared. I'll shoot off a text to Rider and Stoke, tell them to camp at my place." Rush glanced at Camille from the corner of his eyes. "I don't think she's up to anything this time. But we'll know more once we hear what she has to say. She agreed to give us her full cooperation in exchange for protection."

Moss gave him a friendly slap on the back. "Your call, buddy. Gonna be a tough sell to the family, though."

"I know. Just didn't have the heart to tell her *no*."

"Are you sure you're not letting your personal feelings cloud your judgment? Camille is the reason you ended up with Halo. Are ya hoping to rekindle the sparks between Camille and Rebar?"

"I didn't go looking for the woman," Rush said irritably. "But if her breakup with Shade is the real deal this time, we'll find out for sure if Rebar is truly over her. Would be a nice bonus if Rebar moved on with Camille, don't ya think?"

Moss raised his hands in surrender. "You're playing with fire, man. I'll help you with mission-based tasks but I'm staying out of this drama."

"Fair enough." Rush beckoned Camille over with a nod. "Hop on back with me. The guys will bring your car over after it's scanned."

"Scanned for what?" she asked. "Where are we going now?"

"Anything suspicious. We try to keep stalkers away from my ranch. I won't put anything past Shade or Malika at this point."

"Okay." She climbed onto the passenger seat and settled in.

Moss had already given a farewell nod and retreated to his house. Rush realized that by bringing Camille home he'd sparked tension within the group. He wondered how Rider and Stoke would react? If they supported his decision, the others would follow suit, except for Shook. He seemed firm on the matter. Still, he could maybe be swayed if Rider and Stoke were agreeable.

*Will they support my decision or feel the same as the others?* Rush hoped Camille's cooperation would soften their attitude toward her. Moreover, he hoped she had valuable information that would validate taking her under their wing.

Everything about this could blow up in his face if Camille turned out to be a mole sliding into their ranks. Despite the risk, Rush couldn't turn her away. She was a carbon copy of Cameo, and in an inexplicable way he found comfort in her presence.

*My curiosity about Cameo's twin may be my undoing,* he inwardly worried. Regardless, he'd made an independent choice and he'd have to own any repercussions that arose.

"Hold on tight," he told her, then fired up the engine. "There's a helmet on the backrest, put it on."

Rush spotted Stoke and Rider waiting at his garage when he arrived at his sprawling ranch about thirty minutes later. He pulled up next to them. Their faces brightened upon his approach.

"You found Halo!" Stoke hopped off his bike. "Where'd you run off to, girl?"

Camille pulled her helmet off and slid off the bike. "Sorry to disappoint you, guys. I'm the evil twin." She laughed.

Rider and Stoke shot Rush a guarded look.

"Long story," he told them. "I'll fill you in after we get her settled. Levi and Moss are bringing her car over after they scan it."

"You brought Halo's sister here?" Rider scoffed with a laugh of disbelief. "Are you crazy, man?"

"Maybe." Rush got off the bike.

"What about Rebar? How's this gonna affect him?" Stoke asked.

"I haven't thought everything through yet, okay?" Rush

grumbled. "I've been on the road nonstop since last night. My balls are still vibrating, and I'm tired. Chill, okay?" He grabbed Camille's hand and stalked off toward the house. "We'll work it out somehow," he hollered back to them.

"Damn," Rider muttered. "This is gonna get messy."

"No doubt." Stoke agreed. "Can't believe he brought that bitch back here."

Rider chuckled sarcastically. "He may as well invite Malika, too. Then we'll have a real party."

"I can hear you," Rush growled from several feet ahead.

The four of them gathered in the living room. Camille sat beside Rush on the sofa. She toyed with frayed threads on her tattered jeans. He presumed the jeans were supposed to look ragged by the placement of the holes. She seemed nervous, and rightfully so, by the reaction of his friends.

"Didn't think we'd see *you* again," Stoke told her. "We heard you weren't very nice to Halo at Amarillo after she saved your ass."

"You're right. I wasn't," Camille admitted. "She was amazing. Not only did she risk her own safety to help me, but she was so forgiving afterward. She was the same way the first time we met. She and Rebar drove down to my garage. That's how she ended up with the Gran Sport. She wanted to get to know me, but I was a bitch then, too. I was jealous of her relationship with Rebar, not so much that she had him but that they shared a deep love."

Rush tensed and masked his feelings by checking his phone. The last thing he wanted to hear was how much Cameo and Rebar loved each other.

"You're not shy, are ya?" Rider smirked.

"No. Sorry. Is my sister?"

"I wouldn't say she's shy, just more reserved among strangers," he replied.

Stoke leaned back in a cushioned armchair and stretched

his legs. "Then tell us why you're really here. I've got a few suspicions. You could be running interference for Malika, hoping to make another play for Rebar, or coming in as a mole for all we know. Since you're not shy, give us the lowdown, Camille. What's your agenda this time?"

"And don't act dumb," Rider added. "We know you're a registered nurse with advanced education, and that you restore classic cars. You're far above average intelligence and we've been around the block a time or two."

Rush glanced at her. Previous visible apprehension simply melted away as her mood shifted and she started talking. She didn't seem rattled at all as she told them everything she'd seen and then heard between Shade and Malika from the other side of the bedroom door. If anything, she sounded full of rage and disgust.

Her cool composure made him realize that though she was identical in appearance to Cameo, they differed in personality. This woman emanated an air of confidence that paralleled his own. Rush could visualize Camille fearlessly tending Shade's gator bite down in the bayou.

He recalled how nervous Cameo had been upon meeting his friends. And the night Rider inadvertently triggered a PTSD episode, sending Cameo running into the lake.

Though White Wolf had stated that Cameo shadowed her mother's Lakota spirit, Rush noticed a strong resemblance in aura between Camille and Malika. Then again, Cameo had been nothing less than a warrior against the General. She exhibited courage and fortitude as he'd never seen in a female.

Still, Camille carried an edge he hadn't noticed in her twin, which helped him understand how this one was able to manipulate Rebar and drive Cameo away.

"Are you hungry, thirsty?" Rush asked when she'd finished giving them a detailed account of Malika and Shade.

"I am," she replied.

"I can make you a sandwich or something," he offered.

"Whatever you have is fine. I'm not a picky eater. Down in the bayou we survived on wild honey, figs, and crawfish." She sounded amazingly casual about it.

"Will you tell us about the Louisiana abduction?" he asked, hoping she'd regale them. "We've only heard bits and pieces passed on by Chamber."

She gave him a cutting look. "You want to hear how I met Shade?"

"Actually, how you and two chicks managed to kidnap him," Rush replied. "We're not fans of the man."

"Unless it's too painful to relive," Rider added.

"No, I can talk about it. If it'll help you feel better about me, I'd like to set the facts straight. Nobody's ever asked for my side of the story."

"Let me grab you a bite first." Rush hurried into the kitchen and peered into the fridge. He hadn't time to shop. They'd just returned home yesterday. He stared at the lone leftover Ribeye and potato salad. He hoped she meant what she said about not being picky. He popped it in the microwave then spooned potato salad onto the plate, grabbed a bottled water and walked back to the living room. "This is all I have right now. We just got back into town yesterday. Sorry."

"Mm. Looks delicious. Shade and I cooked out on the grill almost every night. I'm more of an outdoors type. I'll miss the motocross track he built. I was getting good at racing." She shrugged while eating. "My garage, too. I used my own money to build it. He's going to have to reimburse me for what I have in the place. I inherited a nice chunk from Jared and used much of it to get my garage up and running. I didn't want to depend on Shade for money. I've always been independent."

"You're serious about leaving him this time?" Stoke pried.

Camille scoffed between bites. "Hell yeah. I played along

with his twisted scheme to seduce Rebar. I sank to a new level of low. I didn't think I could do worse than jabbing Shade's butt with sedative and helping those two nutjobs drag him to Joan's shed in the bayou. But I surprised myself. Got caught up in Shade's thirst for revenge against Rebar for leaving and taking some of the guys with him. We were all sad when Talon, Kohl, and Chamber left."

Incredulity swept over Rider's face. "Why'd you do it then? Why'd you agree to hurt your sister that way?"

"Jealousy, I guess. She was in a loving relationship, and I wasn't. Plus, I was on Shade's side, angry that Rebar took half the troop with him. After they left, nothing felt the same. Rebar ruined our perfect family. Shade convinced me that he needed to pay."

"Seems you're easily swayed to do others' bidding," Rider pointed out. "You let Joan bribe you into kidnapping Shade, then let him persuade you into going after Rebar. Makes me wonder whose side you'll be on next."

She nodded and shrugged. "I get why you'd think that. I'm not asking you to trust me. I'm sure my sister won't be happy that I'm here. I need protection, though. And that is what Ricochet is about, isn't it? Helping women get out of bad situations?"

"Yeah," Rush replied.

"And my sister is missing, is that right?"

"Not missing. Just taking some time to relax," Stoke replied, with a look of caution at Rush.

Rush picked up on the guys' concern that he was getting too friendly with Camille.

Camille frowned. "Rush said nobody knows where she went."

Rider sighed. "Rush talks too much. You just mind your manners and let us worry about Halo."

Camille polished off the steak and potatoes then set her

plate aside. "All I need is some help until I get a lawyer to retrieve my assets. I was raised in a family of attorneys. Jared's top man said if I ever needed anything, to let him know. I just need protection until this Shade-Malika thing is over. I'll pay you if that's what it takes. I have money."

"We don't take money from rescues," Rush told her. "All the men in Ricochet have good jobs."

"So will you help me?"

"Yeah," Rush replied, not giving Stoke or Rider an opening to object. He was intrigued by this woman. "Will you tell us about the bayou?"

"If I must." She rolled her eyes with a light laugh.

Stoke pushed off the chair. "I've heard all I need to know. I'm hitting the sack."

Rider followed his lead. "We'll camp out back tonight. Our gear is still on the bikes from the trip to Pine Ridge."

# CHAPTER SIX

Disappointment fell over Rush. He'd hoped Camille's candor would win them over. After all, she was more than willing to chatter about anything to ease their minds. He imagined reliving her hellish ordeal in Louisiana couldn't be easy, yet she'd seemed totally agreeable. She'd graciously fielded their intrusive questions and didn't appear one bit evasive.

"Levi and Moss should be by soon," Rush said. "I'll unlock the garage for them. Catch you guys in the morning."

They gave him a nod then strolled outside toward the parked bikes. He realized that his decision to help Halo's twin was not going over well at all, despite Camille's eager cooperation. He didn't know what it would take for the others to get onboard with the mission. Thus far, not one member had reacted with a hint of positivity. Given that, he could only imagine Rebar's thoughts on the matter.

*Or . . . could Rebar be the one to sway them? If Rebar still has a soft spot for Camille, he could be the answer to my dilemma.*

His thoughts flipped back to Santa Fe and how he felt fate might have intervened, that there was a reason Camille had walked into the cantina minutes after they had. No way could she have known they'd be there.

"Do you wanna hang out at the garage with me until Moss and Levi get here with your car?" He didn't feel comfortable leaving her alone in his house.

"I'd love to see your garage. Looks like I'll have to start over or give up my dream of working on cars and just stay with nursing. I'm taking classes so I can go back for my doctorate."

He studied her face for a few moments. "Education is good to have. But I'd hate to see you lose your dream." He took her plate to the sink. "C'mon. I'll show you where we'll keep your car."

They strolled down the path to his garage. He keyed the lock and led her inside then flicked on the overhead lights.

"Wow . . ." Camille wandered from car to car. "These are all yours?"

"Most of them. Some are waiting to be picked up."

"You flip cars, too?" she asked with a curious tilt of her head.

He laughed a little. "Not hardly."

"Do you find them at auctions?"

"No. I have a business. People hire me to restore their finds. I rarely frequent auctions."

"You must have an impressive reputation. No one has come to me yet. I still find my projects at auction then flip 'em. I'm trying to build my business. I also just started taking classes. School's only been back in session for a week . . ." She roamed around his garage looking at everything from floor to ceiling. "Can't say my mind is geared for school right now. I was only doing it to please Shade anyway."

He followed her as she inspected every car. "Don't you wanna be a nurse anymore?"

"Not really." She shrugged. "It was a great paying job, but I was really burnt out after fifteen years in skilled care. Then I pulled that stunt with Joan and Missy. That really put a black mark on my resume even though the State Board didn't yank my license."

"Sorry to hear that."

"Thanks. I just need to figure out my next move. I have money, and a good attorney should be able to help me retrieve all my assets from Shade's property. Sure glad I didn't marry him. I'd have lost it all." She stopped to admire his Mercury Montego. "Don't see many of these around. Nice car."

"Thanks. This one's mine."

She turned toward him just as a car rumbled up the drive.

"Sounds like Moss and Levi with your Shelby." He walked to the door and pushed the button to let them in. The garage door groaned a little as it opened. He looked up and noticed a bent track. "Looks like that tornado left some minor damage. I'll have to get on that in the morning. I need to check the roof, too. May be loose tiles up there." He waved the guys in.

Moss waited outside on his Harley while Levi pulled Camille's car in and parked it beside the Montego.

"Did you find anything?" he asked Levi.

Levi shook his head. "Nope. Clean as a whistle."

"Good job. Thanks, mate."

"No worries." Levi gave Camille a once over. "Huh. Mind-blowing. Like looking at a mirror image." He turned toward Rush. "I gotta run. It's late. Are you heading back out in the morning to search for Halo?"

Rush inwardly cringed. He'd already revealed too much. "I'm sure she'll be back soon," he told him.

Levi looked at him strangely but didn't push. "Alrighty then. Catch you later."

"Thanks, Levi." He watched him hop on back with Moss, gave a wave then closed the door.

Camille didn't miss a beat. "You all seem to have mixed viewpoints on where my sister is. Is she missing or not?"

"She's fine." He circled her car, doing a thorough visual inspection over, under, and inside.

"Afraid they missed something?" she asked.

"I'm not afraid of anything." He finished his search then returned to face her. "Don't forget that. The only reason I'm using caution is to protect your ass. Shade and Malika don't intimidate me."

"You are a hardass, aren't ya?" She moved toward him as he stood with his back toward her car.

"Nah. Just don't bow to fear." He tried to avoid eye contact.

"Hm. I bet you have a weak spot," she purred, sweeping all that long blonde hair back with one hand. For a split second he saw Cameo. The resemblance was uncanny, right down to some of their hand movements. "You have no idea where my sister is, do ya?"

"That . . . is not your concern. You're here for one reason and one reason only, to stay safe until Shade and Malika are no longer a threat. They want war on Ricochet, it'll be the last war they wage."

"I can see why Cameo left Rebar for you." She gave him a slow once-over. "You're just all hard male through and through."

"Check your facts, babe. Rebar threw her away for you," he reminded her, feeling uneasy at her proximity.

"I don't see a mechanic's pit or workstations in here. Do you have another building?"

"You're inquisitive, ya know that?" He dipped one brow.

She smiled. "That's your polite way of saying I'm nosy, right?"

"And sharp," he added with a scoff.

"How long has Cameo been missing? Does anyone have a clue to her whereabouts?"

Rush sighed and gave up trying to dodge her questions. "Last we heard she was in Austin. She's independent. I'm sure she's safe and on her way back any day. Everyone needs time alone now and then."

"Agreed. But in this case, I sense an urgency. You act like you're not worried but it's all over your face." She leaned closer. "You *are* afraid. You're worried she ran back to Rebar."

"Do you know something I don't?" He cast a probing look.

"Only that they love each other. I don't know my twin very well, but she seems a bit too refined to fit in down here with all these roughnecks."

"She's doing just fine."

"Keep telling yourself that, Rush. Maybe one day you'll believe it. You made your move on her in Santa Fe, didn't you?"

He forced a smug grin to hide his shock. "There you go sticking your nose again where it doesn't belong."

"I was there, remember? I tried tending your wound. I saw the way you and Cameo kept looking at each other. I know all about hooking up in desperate situations. You wanted to know about the bayou, right?"

He nodded.

"I'll tell you." She hopped effortlessly onto the hood of her car. "Come here. I won't bite." She took his hand and pulled him closer.

"Just the narrative version, babe. No need to act it out." He shot her a warning look.

"Oh don't be such a baby." She took his other hand and held them in hers, then began telling her story from the day Joan blackmailed her to the end.

In extensive detail, Camille opened up about her horrific ordeal that began in Houston and ended in the swamps of Louisiana. Not once did she break down while divulging everything she and Shade had endured. However, when she spoke of how she fell in love with Shade, tears pooled in her sultry blue eyes. She truly had loved the man.

When she finished, they were quiet for a while, taking it all in.

Rush wiped a tear from her cheek. He couldn't help but feel sympathy for this beautiful woman with the heart of a lioness. The way she'd saved Shade's life was nothing short of heroic. He understood how easily people could fall from grace and into situations beyond their control.

He replayed her story in his head. She was so much like Cameo, only in a different setting. They both had skill, tenacity, and extraordinary survival instincts. Neither got rattled in extreme situations. Camille had saved Shade. Cameo had saved *him*. And both had fallen into the arms of the men they helped. Both girls loved muscle cars, though Camille's passion in that area went further. They were sassy, strong, and undeniably sexy. Twins who survived brutal childhoods and rose above the din of their past to success.

"I guess that made it easier for you to pick up vibes from me and Cameo. You were in a similar situation."

"Yeah. I don't fault you," she replied gently. "But you gotta know, Cameo's in love with Rebar. What happened between you and her was two people seeking comfort in dire circumstances. You keep pulling and she'll pull back. She's strong."

He lowered his eyes, feeling the truth weigh in like heavy chains. "You're more like her than you want to admit. You're both incredibly strong females. You saw her, she fights like a wildcat."

"She's tough, that's for sure. But we're not alike. She'll analyze her situation every which way possible and probably end up where she started anyway. I'm not analytical. And . . . I wasn't bound to anyone when Shade and I fell into each other's arms."

He raised his head so that their eyes met. "Be careful about calling the kettle black, babe. You bedded Rebar and broke them up."

"True." She shrugged. "But I figured she'd run to you, and I was right."

"How do you do that?"

"What?"

"Make everything sound like simple logic?"

"Just how I am. I don't overthink things."

"Obviously." He scoffed.

"Hey. Had I not met Shade, I'd still be working the double shifts, and it was backbreaking work. We were always under-staffed. Even though I gotta get through this heartbreak, I'm better for it. I have a fat inheritance, a new dream, and well . . . hopefully soon, a place to live."

"You can stay with me until then. Makes no sense sending you out as a target after all they put you through."

"That's the first time I've told anyone the whole story since my talks with Rebar. He was the only one who got me back then. He was in the war, you know. He understood the trauma. We used to sit on the porch and talk for hours. When he left, that's what I missed most."

"What's so special about that guy?" Rush couldn't grasp the hold his half-brother had on these women. "He's a social recluse who spends all his time inventing things."

"Rebar's a sweet guy. He's not always reclusive. Okay, well, maybe he is," she agreed with a delicate laugh. "He gets the PTSD. He lives with it."

"But Cameo didn't have that before she met him."

"How do you know? She endured cruel whippings as a child then was sent away to be raised by strangers. I'm guess-ing she had PTSD all her life but never knew it until all these triggers brought it to the surface."

Rush wrinkled his brows. "Then why . . . why have you been so mean to her?"

"It wasn't intentional. She burst into my life wanting me to reconcile with a terrorist . . . my mother. My relationship to Shade was feeling shaky. Then one day, in walks my stunning twin, flaunting Rebar on her arm, and driving my dream car."

"You got the car," he reminded her. "Wasn't that enough?"

"I don't hate her. She just rubbed me the wrong way. I can't explain it." She sighed in open frustration. "Can we talk about anything but Cameo?"

"If we don't mention the name Rebar again," he countered. She laughed. "Touché."

"Glad that's settled," he said with a grin.

She surprised him by wrapping her long denim covered legs around the back of his and tugging him closer. "I have an idea, Rush Levvy." She curled her arms around his neck. "Let's forget everything for tonight."

He pulled his head back with a wary look. "You're dangerous."

"Tell ya what, sexy. You pretend I'm whoever you want me to be, and we can get lost in that." She wriggled her body against his, positioning herself just right on the hood of her car. "Just so you know . . . I'm not rebounding. I'm so over the men who hurt me. I'll get my money, my cars, and my life back on track. I only need a little help along the way." She dropped one hand to his waist and undid the fly to his jeans. "And tonight, you're exactly what I need."

He moved to back away, but she slipped that dainty hand down his pants and lifted her shirt. He sucked in a sharp breath at her touch and his focus went to her braless chest.

"Remember, gorgeous, I'm whoever you want me to be right now, right here. Nobody needs to know," she whispered against his ear.

Her sensual taunt sent an ache straight to his groin. She began kissing his neck, then tongued his ears. He was quickly coming undone. Closing his eyes, he leaned into her and let that hand caress him into full arousal.

"Hell with it," he muttered, then lifted her off the hood long enough to tug her frayed jeans down. She wore only a strip of lace as panties. He didn't bother fussing with them but simply ripped them off with one hand then plopped her back on the car.

"Better," she purred while sliding his jeans down, then pushing his T-shirt up and off. She tossed it on the floor.

She tried to kiss his lips, but he hedged her attempt. If this seductive wild thing wanted to forget everything, he'd grant her that. He'd give her a ride she'd never forget and ease his own agony as well. But he'd never trust his heart to such a vamp.

Camille had broken his resistance. He blocked out emotion and tuned in to raw physical need. Her floral scent, satiny skin, silky hair. The sound of her voice coaxing him on.

He'd kept his libido under control to give Cameo time, to not pressure her. But cold showers weren't cutting it lately, with her living in his house, physically within reach but emotionally not ready. She showed no signs of wanting to take things to the next level.

And tonight, he had no idea where she was, when she'd call, or who she was with. *Tonight is what is.* And throwing herself at him right now was a foxy clone of the woman he loved. Tonight, he'd slake the burning need he'd iced for weeks.

He allowed her to kiss him everywhere but his lips to avoid emotional entanglement. If she wanted comfort, wanted his body, fine. He'd surrender to his primal urges for just tonight. She laid back on the car, gazing up at him with sheer desire. He flattened his palms against her bare skin and moved them over her flat stomach then upward.

She opened herself to him. No inhibitions. No doubt. The woman wanted his body. If she wanted more, she'd be sorry. He gripped her hips with both hands and slid her closer then plunged deep into her wanton heat.

She gasped and stared up at him. "Feel good?"

He didn't reply but drove deeper until she laid flat out panting for breath, writhing, and moaning on the hood of her fine car. He never let up. If this arrogant temptress dared to command the fire she'd started, he'd show her just who had more control. He had more than enough stamina to wear out even the saltiest wench.

Closing his eyes, he forced Cameo from his mind. He refused to let Camille manipulate his thoughts. She'd played on his vulnerability to have her way. But he'd never disrespect Cameo by pretending this woman was her. He was not making love to a surrogate despite Camille's head games.

This was just one night—one night of much needed physical release from stressful days on the road and emotional turmoil.

An unpleasant thought blazed into his mind. He'd judged Rebar for succumbing to this very same female. The reality seared his brain, his soul. Still, Rush wasn't about to make the same mistake probie had made. He'd never send Cameo packing to shack up with this woman.

*No. I'm nothing like my half-brother.*

Morning dawned with Camille coiled around him in his bed. What he swore would be only one night, had transformed into a marathon of unbridled passion. She had more stamina than he ever deemed possible. Now he understood how she was able to help Shade survive the swamps.

Somewhere in the night, they'd moved from the garage to his bed. He was exhausted. Hadn't slept much in days. Even so, he'd not let this woman outdo him.

"Shade must've been starving you," he murmured as she straddled his waist.

"You have no idea," she said on an airy breath. "And you are precisely what this nurse prescribed to ease my torment. My gosh, I can't believe Cameo ever let you out of bed."

"We haven't . . . she's not . . ." He sighed. "Never mind."

"She hasn't let you make love to her yet? And she's living with you?"

"She's been traumatized and needs time to heal." He wondered who he was trying to convince, himself or the she-devil on top of him.

"Uh-huh. You're a really bad liar." Camille scoffed. "Their first week together, my twin had Rebar for breakfast, lunch, and dinner. I would know. I dropped in on him and there she was, wearing only his shirt. I was shocked over how quickly they fell into bed. Rebar was always cautious with his heart."

He cocked a brow. "Is this your idea of pillow talk?"

"I'm sorry. I can be rather blunt. Sure does explain our incredible night together." She dragged her finger leisurely down his chest. "A stud like you needs to be taken care of. And I'm all about taking care of people in need," she purred. "Seems we've both been starving."

He couldn't withhold a grin. "Shut up, woman. Get back to it. I might be tired but never too tired."

"Mm . . . my kinda man." She lifted her hair with both hands then let it fall around her shoulders in waves of golden shimmer, reigniting the ache in his groin for more.

His body responded fervently to every move she made, every touch, every look from those enchanting eyes. If ever a woman was skilled in the art of pleasing a man—it was this one.

# CHAPTER SEVEN

"Hello, is this Cameo Parker?" asked a man when she answered her cellphone.

"Yes." Her nerves bristled at a stranger's voice, wondering who had found her and how. She'd done a fairly decent job covering her tracks by using only cash and making just the one call to Shook. She squinted at her phone. *Eight in the morning. Ugh.* "Who's this?"

"My name is Johnathan Grayson, attorney for the late Congressman Jared Connor. I've been trying to reach you for over a year."

"I've only been back in America since May. How'd you get this number?"

"It wasn't easy. But after General's Fritz's death, contact information for all relatives was released to interested parties," he told her. "I've called your phone every day since."

Cameo tensed. She checked her spam log. Sure enough, this number was on the list. "I'm not related to that man."

"That is not why I am calling. I'm acting on behalf of Jared Connor. I have your address listed as Denver. How soon can you come to my office in Austin, Texas?"

"Your office is in Austin?" She wondered if it was coincidence or if someone was trying to lure her into the open. Had Shook disclosed her location? Too many questions and no answers. She hated that she'd become fearful. This was never her way. When she first met Rebar, she was cocky and fresh.

"Yes, Ma'am." He gave her the exact address. "Are you able to get here this week by chance? I'm retiring at the end of

August and would be very relieved to handle this personally, as per Jared's wishes."

"Let me guess. When I get there the whole Ricochet crew will be waiting." She sighed.

"Excuse me? I'm afraid I don't know what you're talking about." He sounded sincere.

Knowing it would take the guys about two hours to get there, she decided to throw a wrench into this obvious ploy. "You know what, I'm on my way out of town. I can swing by your office within the hour. Otherwise, whatever business you have with me will have to wait." *There,* she thought. *If anyone from Ricochet thinks I'll give them a heads up by making an appointment, they've got another thing coming.*

"Well, I suppose I can rearrange my schedule. This shouldn't take long."

"I'm sure it won't." She sighed.

*If Rush is this determined to find me, I may as well face him. Don't know what I'll say. He'll have questions that I have no answers to.*

She realized she'd agreed to be his girlfriend way too soon. But at the time, it felt right. They were cozy and romantic, and he'd slid into her life smoothly at the perfect moment.

"I'll text you the address. See you soon then?" the man asked.

"Yes." She ended the call.

A text came through with a city address and the firm's name. Grayson and Ferguson, attorneys at law. Maybe it wasn't a ploy by Rush after all. But why agree to meet with me this early in the morning?

After brushing her hair and teeth, she pulled on the black leather pants, cropped white tee and Rebar's leather riding jacket. She never thought to grab a change of clothes before bolting from Rush's house. She just needed to get away. And her extra emergency bag was still in storage. She laced up the leather boots, gathered her things and trotted down to the checkout desk.

"How was your stay?" A young man asked as he took her key card and looked her up and down. Normally, she'd have something flippant to say in response to his obvious gesture. Not today. She just wanted to get moving.

"Everything was good, thank you." She paid with cash, stole a peek outside then dashed to her car. Nobody seemed to have tracked her down yet.

*Ha, maybe I'm giving myself too much credit here. They may not even be looking for me.*

She punched the address into the GPS. A short drive later, she arrived at a professional building. Before walking in, Cameo checked the sign mounted to a stone wall to be sure the attorney's name was listed. Sure enough, it was. She stole into the building, keeping a watchful eye on all corners. To her relief, she made it to Grayson's office without passing anyone, not even a janitor.

*Everyone's probably still in bed,* she mused, wishing she were, too. *But better to get this out of the way early so I can get on my way.*

"Ms. Parker, a pleasure to finally meet you," a short, white-haired man wearing an expensive-looking suit said, offering his well-manicured hand in greeting. "Please, come in and sit down. May I get you coffee, tea, or juice?"

"No, thank you. I don't have much time."

"Very well, then." He gestured for her to sit in a finely upholstered chair near a giant L-shaped oak desk. After she sat, he walked around to his chair, placed a pair of wire-rimmed glasses on his nose and took a seat in a high-back brown leather office chair. "This is for you. I was instructed to deliver this in person to you and only you." He slid a large manila envelope across the desk.

"What is it?"

"A DVD and a key. I was not permitted to view the DVD. I respect my clients' wishes," he told her.

"That's all?" She blinked in surprise. This was much easier than anticipated.

"If you'll be so kind as to sign this document stating that you received the contents, that will be all." He smiled cordially. "You may watch it in my private office or at your leisure. With this I'll be able to close the file on Congressman Jared Connor's estate."

"You met his other daughter, too, didn't you?" she pried.

"I cannot say. I'm sorry. Client privacy laws." He smiled again.

"I'm not sure when I'll have access to a DVD player." Then she thought about Rebar's house. He had every device imaginable. However, Denver was fourteen hours away by car. And Chamber would probably be there. She had no idea what message the father she'd never known had left for her. She wanted utter privacy when she found out, and she'd prefer to be alone. She looked at Grayson. "If you don't mind . . ."

"Say no more." He rolled away from the desk and sprang lightly to his feet for an old guy. He motioned her with a sweep of one arm to a closed door. "Nobody will hear or disturb you in there."

Cameo nodded respectfully then walked into the room. Grayson closed the door behind her. She glanced around the cozy office. An entertainment center spanned the entire length of the main wall. To her left were overstuffed leather chairs in each corner with a tall potted tree and a window between them. On her right was another wall decorated with medals and plaques. She wandered over and saw that Grayson was a decorated war hero.

She wondered when he'd had time to achieve all that and law school, too. If he was Jared's right-hand man, did he also know the General? *I'm overthinking.* She blew out a breath. *Just watch the damn video and get out of here.* She was definitely curious about the father she'd never met.

A wireless DVD player had been placed on the table. She pulled up a chair, sat down and pushed the open button then unsealed the envelope and removed the silver disc. "Okay, old man. Let's see what words of wisdom you left for your other daughter." She leaned back after pressing play on the remote.

"Hello, Cameo. We meet at last," said a white-haired man from a large tufted burgundy Queen Anne style wing-back chair. His blue eyes carried dark shadows, sending chills down her arms. Her first instinct was to run, but she felt frozen in place, compelled to hear his words.

"I'm sorry you're the last to hear from me. Old Fritzy must be dead if you're viewing this. Grayson had strict instructions to hold this video in his safe until that bastard was gone, in order to protect you." He paused and just stared into the camera for a minute before continuing. "I wish I could see you all grown up. I bet you're stunning like your sister. I heard you took a job caring for animals. You and Camille, so much alike yet polar opposites in many ways. I'm sure you're wondering why I left you this DVD." He stopped talking to take a pill.

"Get on with it already," she mumbled.

"First, forget all the lies Malika Rain or Montana Parker or whatever name she goes by these days, has fed you. She's a scheming, wicked wench who cares only for herself. Now, what I'm about to tell you, only three people before you know. Those three people are the General, Malika, and me. Please be sure to sit before listening further." He paused and waited as if he were in the room.

"Okay. I'm already sitting. Keep going." She felt ridiculous talking to a dead man. She studied his face, noting the square chin, thin lips, and wrinkles all over. This was her biological father. He didn't look impressive. He was just a little old man rambling on. She'd wasted too much time wondering about nothing. She was about ready to get up and walk away when his next words gripped her attention like a steel vice.

"Malika is not your mother," he said. "She and the General, or Fritz as I called him, ran a human trafficking ring out of a remote dusty town in Amarillo. How was I involved you ask? I owed Fritz big time. To say he owned me is an understatement. He paved my way up the political ladder, then threatened to have me disbarred and imprisoned if I ever crossed him. He and Malika fabricated a story about you and Camille to cover their asses. Fritz kept Malika in hiding for six months to convince everyone she was pregnant. Then at a planned time, they filled out fake birth certificates stating that Malika birthed twin girls."

Cameo gasped in shock. She gripped the table edge with both hands to steady herself. As if knowing she'd need a moment, Jared had stopped speaking. *Why me?* She wondered. *Why didn't he tell Camille? Why'd he wait so long?* Her mind swam with confusion.

"I'm sorry to lay this on you, dear one. But I could not trust Camille because of her involvement with Shade. If she told Shade, he'd never let her tell anyone. His loyalty to Fritz is disturbing. I never did understand it. And I want both my girls to know the truth. Therefore, I had to trust you. Back to the point, I *am* your father. However, I don't know where your mother is. I'll do my best to explain what happened. I was married, with four sons, working my way up to the White House. I was a struggling attorney when I met Fritz. He was a four-star General with serious clout. We became friends and he used his contacts to launch my career. In politics, you need money and connections to get anywhere."

Jared stopped suddenly for a moment. He looked abruptly off camera and cocked his head. Less than a minute later, he resumed.

"Sorry. I thought I heard someone. Anyway, I was on my way up. Thought I had it all, a wife, four intelligent sons, a promising career . . . then I met *her* . . . the loveliest creature God ever created. She breezed into my office one day as a temp secretary. I hired her immediately as my personal fulltime assistant. She was bright, witty, and absolutely stunning with long ebony black hair and eyes like rain. And most of all, she listened to me. Not like my spoiled, whiny, money-grubbing wife who never heard a word I said. No . . . Feather was dropped straight from Heaven. She had a genuine kindness that is rare. I wanted her more than anything. She was quite a bit younger than I was, but her parents didn't mind. I promised to marry her the minute I got free. I was boxed in pretty heavily by Fritz at the time."

He grabbed a tissue from his desk and blew his nose then pinched the bridge of his nose before continuing.

"And that's why I saved this video for you. I hope one day you will return and have questions. I suspect Fritz and Malika are onto me wanting to tell my girls the truth about their mother. I don't want to invade your life or risk your safety by tracking you down. So, I'm making this tape just in case anything happens before you decide to seek answers, if ever. Your mother, your real mother, may still be alive. She was only seventeen when she had you and Camille."

Cameo had to pause the DVD. She dropped her head in her hands and sobbed. Everything she thought she knew was a lie. She wasn't sure she could handle much more. Yet this man, this feeble old man, had taken the time to make a recording and save it exclusively for her because he couldn't trust Camille. She yanked several tissues from a nearby box and tried to compose herself.

After getting a cold drink from the water cooler, she returned to the TV monitor where Jared's image was frozen on the screen. She wanted to hear about her real mother as painful as it might be. She sat down and with a trembling hand, pressed play.

"I didn't meet Malika until my precious Feather was pregnant. Fritz hired spies to track my every move, and Feather's. I didn't even know Fritz was involved with a woman until he introduced me to that psycho. That's when I learned of their sordid criminal activity. Once they found out Feather was pregnant, they abducted her from the reservation and locked her up with Malika. When you and Cameo were born and they saw how exquisite you both were, they took custody. Fritz took you and told me to raise Camille. But it wasn't that simple. He was a sick man. He had plans to use you the way he did Camille, but you were a hellcat. He said you couldn't be tamed."

Cameo paused the recording again to catch her breath. She and her sister — born into human trafficking. She got out but Camille did not.

She recalled that Camille said she was around eight years old when Jared turned her out. But she thought Jared was the one doing it. Would she gain closure or peace if she knew this awful truth?

Cameo remembered the beatings she took from the General. Brutal, merciless whippings in attempt to subdue her. Then he sent her away at five years old, three years before she'd have been handed over to men for money. Her indomitable spirit had spared her from a worse fate. Compassion for her twin filled her.

As painful as it was, she resumed the video.

"I'm glad you fought him, Cameo, but so very sorry for my cowardice. I was riddled with guilt and grief, terrified of going to prison. He kept the women and girls locked in houses. Men paid big money for a night with Fritz's prisoners. He fed them well, dressed them in the finest clothes and hired people to do their hair and makeup. But the captives were never permitted to leave the house. Fritz gave Feather a choice . . . leave and never return or become one of his whores. They had taken her twins and given her an ultimatum. After six months of terror, she didn't really have a choice. I never saw her again. I'm sure she hates me, and rightfully so."

He held up a key, the same key that she'd pulled from the envelope.

"Write this down, Cameo." He rattled off an address. "You'll know what it's for when you get there. An apology could never be enough for what I've done." He looked to the side again then back at the camera. "Someone's coming. I need to get this in the mail before anyone finds it. Be well, my stunning fiery daughter. If you can manage it, please forgive me for what I've done. I hope the key helps ease your pain. I love you, Cameo."

The video ended abruptly. Cameo grabbed the DVD, address, and key, stuffed them into her purse and ran from the room. She didn't want anyone to see her this way.

Once in her car, she pressed her forehead against the steering wheel while sobbing and shouting her anger to a man who was buried in a grave somewhere. How could she forgive this? He let that vile beast steal his daughters and drive their mother away. She couldn't even fathom their level of evil. Everything she'd heard felt surreal. How could she go to Camille with this? Why did Jared dump the responsibility on her?

*He was a coward. He got that part right.*

In her heart, she knew, even as she wailed her rage, that she'd need to let this go somehow and find peace in order to move on. She felt like a fool for believing Malika's lies.

Everything made sense now. Malika using Camille in her quest for Shade. *That woman never wanted Camille to have Shade.* She was after Shade's empire just like everyone first thought. She deceived and used Camille just as she did anyone who'd further her agenda.

*I wonder if Camille has any suspicions at all toward Malika yet or if she's still blindly following along just as I did.*

Now she understood why Shade and Malika sent Camille after Rebar. They didn't care about anyone's feelings but their own. And if Shade had Malika in his bed, he was the biggest fool of all — or was he?

*After all, he is the General's son. Malika may have met her match tangling with him.*

Cameo had never been able to comprehend her mother's actions. She had done her best by chocking it up to the heart-breaking tale Malika told, about those men stealing her twins and using her as a whore. When in fact, not only had she stolen another woman's babies, but Malika was also using that woman's story as her own.

She wondered what happened to the innocent woman named Feather. Then White Wolf's alarming declaration came to mind. *You're the shadow of Feather Blue.* White Wolf seemed to believe Feather had become a legend, and that Malika was her. What had Malika done to weave such deception that even an old Medicine Man mistook her for Feather Blue?

Almost everything lined up. Feather's disappearance from the reservation, her pregnancy. *How did White Wolf know she was carrying twins? Did he know more than he'd let on? Was this a truth that I needed to find on my own?*

Cameo wished she could pop by his cabin and speak with him, but she had no idea how to find that place on her own. She wondered if he had more information about Feather.

She looked down at the key in her hand, then at the address she'd scribbled onto a piece of paper. She tapped the address into the GPS on her phone. *Waco, Texas.* The fastest route was straight up I-35, only an hour and a half away. And interestingly the midway point between Austin and Dallas.

She wasn't surprised that the attorney and the mystery key were located in Texas. From what she'd learned, Jared was native to the state. Camille had been living near Houston when Joan found her. Shade was a bigwig Texas oil tycoon. The General had set up his trafficking ring in Amarillo, though the man had a mansion in Santa Fe. And of course, Ricochet had to be based in Dallas. Seemed that all the ties to her past were rooted in the Lone Star State.

*Everything happens in Texas.* She sighed. *Not sure I want to stay here anymore.*

# CHAPTER EIGHT

Cameo shifted her car into gear and burnt a trail of rubber leaving the parking lot. First stop — the address Jared had given to uncover what awaited her. She'd laugh at his dramatics if the situation weren't so damn serious. Either way, she wanted to check it out before telling anyone.

She highly doubted he'd left her anything of material value. Her twin had made it clear that Jared left his entire estate to her.

Cameo didn't care about the man's wealth. She wasn't rich nor poor, just somewhere in between.

Her talks with Rebar came to mind. He'd often shared his faith with her. Then she discovered Shook was a Christian, too. Rush had been more reserved about his beliefs. He said he believed in God but never said much more than that.

Maybe God was leading her now. Afterall, by chance she'd hightailed it to Austin to think. Grayson's call was perfect timing. Now she was halfway back to Dallas. Once she investigated this chapter of her life, she was only another hour and a half away from home, well, Rush's home. She thought God might be leading her out of seclusion and back to where she belonged. Back to a man who adored her and had no baggage.

*I ran off without explanation and ignored his calls. I did send word through Shook, though. I do have a right to be alone. But I've been gone long enough. After I see what Jared left for me, I'll drive up and tell Rush what happened.*

She knew he and all of Ricochet would want to know the truth about Malika. This information changed everything.

82

They needed to know that Malika didn't need rescued, that she was a sociopath or worse, just as Shook had warned.

*Yes. I need to speak with Rush about all of this.* Her thoughts began to organize.

The sun beat down from above throwing a glare on the hood of her car by the time she arrived at her destination. She placed her sunglasses in the console and sat still for a few moments staring at the building in front of her.

"A bank," she muttered. "Well, that makes sense. The key is probably for a safety deposit box. Maybe he left me a letter or a document of some type regarding my birthmother." She let out a heavy sigh. Sleep hadn't come easy the past few days. "At least he didn't send me on a scavenger hunt." She had fully expected to arrive at a vacant house as a consolation prize. *Like, hey Cameo, sorry I left everything to my other daughter but here's my summer cabin.*

She wondered how to approach the teller with an anonymous key, especially the way she was dressed. *Gosh. Can this day get any more awkward?* She checked her makeup and hair in the rearview mirror, straightened her clothes, left the black leather jacket in the car, and stepped out into the scorching August heat.

"Hi," she said upon approaching a teller. "My name is Cameo Parker. My father was the late Congressman Jared Connor. He left me this address and key. Is it for a safety deposit box?"

The woman peered over her thick framed glasses with a studious look. "Let me check with the manager. Please wait over there and someone will be with you shortly."

Cameo nodded politely then walked to a small reception area. She filled a paper cup with water from a cooler to quench her thirst. Then another, and another.

"Ms. Parker?" a woman's voice grabbed her attention from behind.

She turned to see a distinguished-looking lady wearing a

skirt suit. Her hair was pulled into a tight bun. Her makeup was minimal and flawless.

"Come with me, please," the woman said.

Cameo followed her through a gate, down a hall and into a windowless room where rows of drawers lined the walls and a metal table sat in the center of the room.

"I checked the documents. I just need to see your photo ID, please."

Cameo pulled her driver's license out. The woman checked it and smiled a business-like smile. "Congressman Connor left specific instructions that if you ever showed up, you were the only one permitted access to this box. She took Cameo's key and one of her own then unlocked a small metal door on the top left corner. The box pulled out like a drawer, it was long and thin.

"I'll leave you alone. When you're finished, please stop by the teller and leave your key as this box will be returned to available status."

"May I ask how long this has been waiting for me?"

"I'm sorry. I can't release that information. I'll give you privacy now. Please accept my condolences on the loss of your father." She offered another plastic smile then exited the small room, closing the door behind her.

She recalled the high-profile case about Jared's suicidal passing. Nobody knew the truth—that Malika killed him. Jared had a criminal past by aiding the General and Malika, even if it was because of blackmail. He should've done the right thing and gone to the law. Instead, he chose money over love.

Both men had paid for their crimes with their lives at the hand of Malika. *One day, Malika will run out of tricks and justice will prevail.* Cameo didn't want to become part of a scandal. Finding her real mother would be a dream come true. And she couldn't be thankful enough to find out none of Malika's blood ran through her veins, or the General's.

"Okay . . ." Cameo drew a deep breath and exhaled, staring at the safety deposit box kept safely hidden for so long, for her eyes only, for however long she did not know. She lifted the lid. "Another envelope. Removing the envelope revealed an aged photo. She picked it up. Though slightly faded with time, the photo was still very clear. "Wow . . . she's beautiful . . ."

She gazed at a woman with raven black hair that carried a rich sheen and cascaded in lovely long waves far past her slender shoulders. She had striking blue slightly elongated eyes. Delicate brows arched perfectly over them.

Cameo couldn't stop gazing at the photo. She touched the photo and traced the woman's outline with her index finger. Tears flooded her eyes. "Mother . . ." Two feathers were tucked into the black tresses. She turned the photo over. Handwritten on the back were the words, *you will always be the love of my life, Feather Blue.*

She clutched the photo to her heart and whispered a prayer request that her mother was alive and well, and that she would find answers about the woman who had birthed her. Birthed them.

She pulled another photo from the box. A young man with blond hair, wearing fringed buckskin pants and shirt, stood beside the raven-haired beauty. She wore an ivory-colored fringed dress adorned with beads, shells, and fringe. They looked happy together. She flipped it over.

*Jared and Feather* was written in cursive on the back.

"Wow, my father had blond hair." She smiled while gazing at them. Then she recalled what the General had said to Malika.

*Every time I looked at the girl all I saw was Jared. Her blonde hair and blue eyes . . . she looked nothing like you. I began to hate her. She became a constant reminder of what he gave you that I could not.*

In all the chaos and then the aftermath, that bit of info he'd dropped hadn't registered . . . until now. Her smile faded. She forced thoughts of that monster from her mind to focus.

There were no more pictures, only a folded piece of letter-size paper. Carefully, she unfolded it and read.

*Dearest Cameo,*

*I'm sorry you never met your mother. I pray there is still time for that to happen. I know Feather would want to know you. You may have been told that I left my entire estate to your twin sister. While I did bestow a sizeable portion of my wealth to Camille, I held back something extra special for you. Inside the sealed envelope is a deed to land in South Dakota. I followed your career from afar. Your love for nature and wildlife would make your Lakota mother and grand-parents proud. I know you'll care for the land and protect it from greedy men who ravage Mother Earth for oil, gas, wood, and gold. I secretly purchased two-hundred acres of beautiful prime land in Sheps Canyon, Hot Springs, South Dakota, to honor Feather. I am confident the spread is a perfect fit for you. Nobody knows I've done this.*

*Now the hard part. I want you to find your mother and make sure she's well cared for. I have no right to ask you. However, I'm appeal-ing to your sense of decency. The land is held in trust for you and Feather as Native Americans therefore is not subject to state or local property tax. I designated you as the trustee. Everything went through all the proper legal channels. Simply present the deed and required ID to the bank listed and the land is yours, signed, sealed, and protected. I'm not trying to buy your forgiveness. I simply want to take care of you and the only woman I ever loved. I pray you find healing, peace, and your mother, after all these years.*

*Love always, your father.*

His signature was scribbled below. Cameo unsealed the fi-nal envelope and read the deed. Her mind reeled. Excitement rose in her spirit. She was filled with astonishment over this turn of events.

Then she thought about Rush. No way would he leave his massive ranch to live with her in South Dakota. She couldn't, wouldn't ignore this opportunity. Having land of her own was a dream come true. She'd be able to continue her work with wildlife and forestry. Seeing her experience, the possibilities were endless.

*I'll still need a job and save up to build a house.* She gathered the documents, secured them in the specially concealed compartment of her bag, dropped the key off with the teller, then left the bank.

She was excited and nervous about telling Rush. How would he react to her moving north? She'd be living ten hours closer to Rebar than to Rush.

If she and Rush were meant to be together, something would work out.

A huge golden sun hung lower in the western sky by the time she left the bank. She veered back onto I-35 and sped north, full of renewed hope for her future. She powered the windows down and basked in the wind whipping her hair. Visions of living off her own land, studying and protecting wildlife, breezed through her mind as she drove.

She'd need to make job hunting one of her top priorities now. Her savings would last only so long, and it wasn't enough to fund a house. *Maybe a trailer for the time being,* she thought. She had enjoyed living in Denver with the cooler climate, the mountains and green rolling hills. From what she'd seen of South Dakota, she felt confident she'd love living there.

A position in Wildlife Management would pay well. With two hundred acres, she might even be able to work for the government on her own land. Finally, one of her dreams felt within reach.

Her thoughts traveled faster than she did on the way back

to Dallas. She tried to imagine what Feather looked like now. Would her mother be happy to see her? Where to begin her search? She wondered if her grandparents might still be alive. How exciting it would be to learn about her true heritage and hear their stories.

She had a lot to consider. As she pulled into Rush's mile-long driveway, the sun barely topped the horizon and streaks of gold, pink and dark blue cast their last rays of daylight across the land. She parked her car where she always had and didn't notice any Harleys sitting in front of the house.

Rush always had company it seemed. Strange that none of the guys were here preparing to grill steaks. She didn't even see Rush's Harley around.

*Maybe he parked it in the garage,* she thought. Feeling a little uneasy, she strolled to the front door and used her key to let herself inside. *Perhaps they're all out on a run together.* She dropped her house key on the table just inside the door.

"Rush?" she called in a normal tone of voice. "Are you here?" *Hm.* No reply. *He must be out riding or hanging with his friends.*

She went to the fridge for a cold drink and noticed there were no groceries. *He hasn't even gone to the store since we returned from Pine Ridge. That's odd.* Then again, the only thing he ever bought was steaks and takeout. *Maybe that's where he is, shopping.*

She spotted his boots near the kitchen door, which led to the patio. She peeked outside to see an empty patio. No signs of life at all. His keys were lying on the counter along with his wallet.

*Nope. Not at the store. Hm.*

He had to be home. She wandered around then headed back to the foyer.

"Rush . . . I'm home," she said. "And I have incredible news. Where are you?" She pushed the bedroom door open. "Ah, he's sleeping." Guilt crept over her. He'd probably been searching for her night and day and finally surrendered to sleep. She felt bad for putting him through it. But the night he accused Rebar of upsetting her, and his jealous attitude had triggered her need to run.

She missed her loft apartment for solitude, so she had done the first thing that came to mind, staying in Austin where they'd shared that thrilling dance.

"Hey, you," she muttered quietly at the bedside, giving him a gentle nudge. "I'm home."

His long lashes fluttered, and he opened his sleepy eyes to look up at her. "Angel, you're back. You worried the hell out of me." He sat up, tangled in the sheets. "Where were you?"

"I stayed in Austin, in that hotel you and I shared. I just needed time to think. I'm sorry for not calling you. I didn't want to argue or feel pressured. I know you've been feeling left out lately. And you seemed jealous of Rebar. There's nothing going on between him and I. We were only talking."

"I know. I'm sorry for behaving like a jealous ass." He glimpsed briefly toward the master bath.

She tilted her head while taking a closer look at the bed, which appeared unusually rumpled. "How long have you been sleeping?"

"I don't know. I was exhausted. We rode out to Santa Fe looking for you. Stoke and Rider went up to Amarillo. Chamber and Rebar went back to Denver, thinking you'd show up there."

"Amarillo? Why on earth would I go there?" She frowned.

"We were just guessing. Never occurred to me that you were only a couple hours away. I should've known you'd check the weather and hunker down."

"You're surprisingly nice about all this. I was worried you'd be furious with me." She glanced around the room.

"Just glad you're home, angel. Don't wanna fight with you. Are you hungry? Let's go out for dinner." He swung his legs over the side of the bed and reached for his jeans.

"I do have some exciting news to tell you. What I found out will affect all of Ricochet. Even if Malika and Shade pursue this crazy war idea, I now know the truth about her."

"I can't wait to hear it." He tugged a shirt over his head. "Where would you like to eat?"

He seemed in a hurry to leave and hadn't even welcomed her with a hug or kiss. She found this unlike him.

"Are you okay?" she asked.

"Yeah. Mind's still groggy from sleeping too long. I'll perk up. Give me a minute to brush my teeth and freshen up, then we can grab some grub. I'm famished."

She plopped down on the bed. "Okay. Go do your thing."

A guarded expression flitted across his face for a split second. She would've missed it had she not been focused on those gorgeous eyes. "I'll make the bed."

"Make the bed," he repeated in a robotic mutter. "Sure. Okay. Yeah." He raked both hands through his mussed black wavy hair.

She watched him intently as he weaved his way to the bathroom. "Are you hungover? Were you partying last night? Because you're definitely not yourself." She began straightening the sheets and shook the blanket to fluff it up.

"I did have a long night, babe. I'll be fine after some fresh air, food, and drink. I've barely eaten a thing in twenty-four hours."

"Are you still angry with me?" she worried.

He turned to look at her. "Angry? No way, angel. I'm thrilled that you came back. It's been a rough few days, is all."

"Aw, I'm so sorry for bolting and putting you through that. I feel terrible. You look shattered."

"You don't owe me an apology. We can talk this out over dinner. I really need some fresh air, babe."

"Okay." She arched her brows with concern but didn't

push further. Clearly, he'd gone through the wringer over her impromptu getaway.

He disappeared into the bathroom. She resumed making the bed. While fluffing the pillows, something shiny flew onto the floor. She reached down and plucked it off the carpet.

*An earring.*

She examined it closely and saw that it definitely wasn't hers.

Her thoughts began rapidly backtracking. He hadn't seemed himself from the moment she'd woken him, his glance toward the bathroom, abnormally tangled sheets, his urgency to get out of the house — she was always too trusting. Assumed he'd been suffering alone in her absence.

She never saw the breakup with Rebar coming either. But he was coerced. Those two women played him to the hilt, manipulating his confused emotions. He was as blindsided as she had been.

Rush, however, had no reason other than lack of self-control. If their budding relationship couldn't withstand a few minor glitches during a period of extenuating circumstances without him jumping into bed with another woman, they certainly didn't stand a chance at the long-term. Even worse, he'd openly pursued her while knowing she was on the rebound.

Now this.

Sadness and anger washed over her. She clutched the earring in a closed fist so tightly the metal cut into her palm. A decision needed to be made.

*Do I confront him or simply walk out the door and never look back?*

He was obviously doing his best to hide it from her. At least Rebar had the guts to break it off face-to-face the honest way. Though it hurt like hell, she could handle that better than deceit. She loathed deception and had hated herself for hiding the kiss with Rush from Rebar. She was glad they'd had a chance to clear the air.

But now she needed to know who had kept her side of the bed warm while she was away trying to sort her thoughts.

# CHAPTER NINE

Quietly she padded to the bathroom and pressed her ear to the door. Muffled voices that she could barely hear, too indistinct for her to discern words but enough to know one of them was a female's voice.

Her nerves were frazzled. She hated this. Last thing she expected was catching Rush with another woman. Today had brought new hope yet also more betrayal. After taking one last thorough look around the room and not finding a single shred of woman's clothing, she knew the *not knowing* would eat at her and never let her go.

*I must know for sure. I need to see his face and who he chose to replace me. Or I'll always wonder.*

Not wanting to appear like a jealous maniac, she pushed the door open slowly. Upon seeing who the other woman was, Cameo flung the door open hard, causing it to bounce off the wall.

Rush and Camille whipped around at the same time, deer in the headlights expressions emblazoned on their faces. Camille wore nothing but one of Rush's shirts.

Cameo should've screamed, or ran, or thrown something — anything but just stand there. However, she couldn't seem to move. The shock of seeing her twin with yet another of her boyfriends propelled her mind into unchartered territory.

"This isn't what it looks like!" Rush blurted out. "We crossed paths by coincidence. She asked for our help. She had nowhere else to stay."

"Funny. I don't see any of the others here. Is this a solo mission, Rush?"

"Nothing happened," he insisted.

Camille let out a huff. "You call last night nothing?"

Frustration creased his face. "I never wanted this to happen. Last night, Moss and Levi scanned her car and hid it in my garage. Camille was feeling down over her breakup with Shade—"

"Ha! You fell for that after she pulled the same routine on Rebar? I thought you were wise to her."

"We really did break up," Camille told her. "I caught Shade in bed with Malika."

"Oh, shut the hell up!" Cameo spat. "I don't believe a word that bleeds from your lying lips."

"It's the truth this time."

"Cry wolf, Camille. Shame on you!"

Rush stepped toward her. "Angel, it was just one night. She was distraught. I had no idea when or if you were coming back. I don't have feelings for her. I'm not Rebar. I don't wanna lose you over one reckless night."

"He's telling the truth," Camille said. "I initiated it. Although I gotta tell ya, sis, you leveled up with this hunk. Rebar was nothing like him. You're one lucky lady to have this stud as your man. I can't believe you've been keeping him on ice. Geez!"

"You told her about our intimate life?" Cameo gasped, glaring at Rush.

"I . . . I may have mentioned something . . . it's not . . . it didn't . . ." he stammered.

Camille laughed. "Intimacy? Don't you mean lack thereof? The man was in serious need. That's the difference between us, sis. I didn't need to think it to pieces like you."

"Maybe because I'm not a man-eating whore like you!" She elbowed Rush out of her way then grabbed Camille by the hair. "Anything else to say before I kick your ass?"

Camille shoved her off. "You're gonna take me on? Try wrestling a three-hundred-pound man into a straitjacket at three a.m. after a double shift in the psych ward."

"Why didn't you just seduce him like you do everyone else?"

Camille's eyes squinted viciously. "You're a clueless spoiled little brat who knows nothing about pleasing a man."

"And you think you're so tough just because you're a nurse?" Cameo hissed. "A tough girl would've put Joan in her place the *first* time she stepped out of line instead of bowing to her demands . . . *fluffy*."

Camille's intensified glare indicated Cameo had struck a raw nerve. "You're not better than me. Just better at hiding the bitch behind your *little miss innocent* act."

"I'd have never slept with your man!"

Camille let out a huff. "You could *never* tempt my man. You can't seem to satisfy *any* man!" Then she belted Cameo across the face. "That's from *fluffy*."

Cameo lost it, simply lost it. She lunged and they began throwing punches, mostly missing each other. Her sister was quite a scrapper. Camille had her by the neck and tried throwing her down.

Rush jumped in to pull them apart. Fight-flight took hold and Cameo saw red. She wrenched free of his grip with an elbow jab to the face.

She made a half-turn then landed a hard side-kick-strike directly to Camille's face. Her head bounced back, she lost her balance and tumbled backward into the tub.

Cameo spun back around, seething at Rush. "Just one night. You threw everything away for just one night with . . . *her*."

With that, she ran from the room, down the hall and slowed down only to grab her bag before racing out the door.

She leapt behind the wheel of her car, keyed the ignition and tore out of there in a flash. Her car windows were still down just as she'd left them.

Had anyone been watching, they'd have seen nothing but a streak of gold flying down his drive.

She never bothered to check for oncoming traffic before hitting the main road doing fifty-five.

Car horns blared. Tires screeched as drivers took action to avoid a crash.

She glanced at the scrambled mass of headlights in her rearview mirror she'd left behind and hoped nobody got hurt. The speedometer needle was bouncing off eighty less than thirty seconds after clearing the chaos she left behind.

She arrived at her rented storage unit fifteen minutes later and parked in the shadows of trees near the building. Sitting in her car, in the dark, with her head resting back against the seat, she let herself cry for the second time today.

Everything in her world had just exploded into an insane miasma of pain and confusion laced with clarity.

A deluge of emotions consumed her thoughts. Their voices rained like fire in her brain.

Rush telling her, *I like Rebar which is why he should never know. We could never be friends because I'm gonna take his woman.*

Rebar's professed intent seeped through her mind — *I love you, doll. You're the one I want.* Then the mind-blowing letdown — *Cameo . . . I still . . . I will always love you. I never lied about that. I called to explain. I've known Camille for a year. I need to give it a shot with her. You deserve a man who isn't torn. I never expected Camille to break it off with Shade. I'm sorry, so very sorry, babydoll.* Followed by his regret . . . *I'm over them but I'll never be over you, babydoll.*

White Wolf's statements echoed through her mind. *A woman who holds her tongue is worth much. I see why the men call you Halo, and why my son is very fond of you. You are half Lakota as is my son. One never knows how the spirits will lead. His* shocking revelation. *I had a feeling you were the lost child of Feather Blue.*

Rush's promise. *I've fallen hard for you, girl. And when the time is right, when you're ready, I'm still gonna make you mine.* Then his calming reassurance. *You are home, angel, you just don't know it yet.*

Cameo scoffed. *Yeah, Rush. I was wise not to sleep with you too soon.*

Shook straight up. *My father was not so far from the truth, hm? Don't ever change, Halo. You have Yeshua. I will subdue Milaka's Lakota magic while you pray to the ultimate power.* Then a confusing statement after that dance. *I told her that I don't love her. My heart is taken. And if I see her again, I won't be so generous.*

And the kicker from Rush *and* Rebar. *Just one night.*

Three extraordinary men. Even through the pain she could still acknowledge their superior characteristics and good looks.

Rebar the genius. Charming and sweet.

Rush, natural born leader of a noble organization.

And Shook—fearless intelligent undercover agent with unique charisma.

She felt strongly connected to all three, though two had betrayed her trust.

Maybe romance wasn't part of her destiny.

In just under four months, she'd struck out twice. Rebar lasted almost two months, chased her down the first week in May, dumped her for Camille the week of July Fourth, her fortieth birthday — *nice gift*. Rush pursued her on her birthday then ended up in bed with her twin six weeks later. The Damocles men had serious issues with fidelity. She surmised both sons were more like their father than they'd ever admit.

Here she was, mid-August, in the middle of a maelstrom of men. She hadn't dated in so long . . . and within a short time of arriving in America, she was entangled in a drama that only belonged in a soap opera on TV.

She couldn't even begin to rehash all the rubbish Camille and Malika had heaped upon her. She felt like the world's biggest fool and if not for this morning's surprise from Jared, she'd be on the next flight to Australia and disappear in the outback at one of her former jobs.

However, now she knew some truths at last. Even better, she had a precious photo of her birthmother and a deed to Native American land in South Dakota. Though her world currently felt shattered, she tried to focus on a new beginning away from Texas, away from Ricochet.

Still, she needed help finding Feather and knew of only one man who might have the compass. But she'd never be able to find White Wolf's cabin on her own. He probably intended it that way to ensure his privacy. *A wise man.*

"Dear God," she prayed. "Thank you for the video from Jared. Please help me forgive him and please, God, help me find my mother."

She sat quietly, waiting for an answer.

*White Wolf.* There was but one person who knew the way to the Medicine Man's cabin.

Cameo doubted Shook would help her since she and Rush were through. Doing so would create conflict within the guys' friendship. She didn't want that even after Rush's heartless betrayal. Rush would receive punishment enough from Camille.

Still, she sensed White Wolf could help, though she couldn't see how. She had to follow her intuition, that little voice inside that wouldn't let go.

She decided to check out the vibes with Shook by sending a text. *Hey. I'm back in Dallas. Can you talk?*

Almost immediately her ringtone sounded. She saw Shook's caller ID flash on her screen. "That was fast," she said.

"We were really worried about you, girl. I'm relieved you're back in town. Have you been to Rush's yet?" His voice carried an air of concern.

"Um . . . yeah. I was there."

"Oh." The call went silent for a few seconds. "Then you know."

"What do I know?" She fished for what he knew.

"That Rush took Camille in until the trouble with Shade and Malika is resolved."

"When did all this take place?"

"Last night," Shook replied. "None of us are onboard with his decision. Levi and Moss dropped her car off last night after scanning it. Rebar and Chamber are staying at his lodge in Denver. Stoke and Rider messaged last night, said things got too heavy for them to handle so they crashed in the yard."

"Stoke and Rider weren't there when I stopped in," she told him.

"I'm not surprised. They probably went home. Nobody wants to help with this one. Camille's trying to win us over but we're not buying her fake charm or damsel in distress routine."

"So, Rush is doing this on his own without support from the others?"

"Seems that way," Shook replied. "We all made it quite clear how we felt, but he's dug in. Took the wench in despite our objections."

"Yeah, in more ways than one. Do you know about their involvement?"

"Whose?"

"Camille and Rush. Did you know they got involved while I was away?"

"Hell no. Who told you that? Camille's only been there for a day."

"I walked in on them, Shook. He tried to hide her, but I found an earring in the bed while he was in the bathroom. He was trying to keep her hidden until he got me out of the house for dinner."

"Are you sure, babe? You didn't misunderstand anything, did ya, hon?"

"Please don't insult my intelligence. I caught them. Rush tried to deny it until Camille opened her trap. They claimed it was one night because they were both distraught. But Camille made sure I knew what a stud he was." She let out a quivering sigh. "One night or one hundred nights . . . doesn't matter. He took her into his bed, then tried to hide it from me."

"Damn him," Shook growled. "I did my best to warn him off her. He simply would not listen. I knew she'd get under his skin. I saw the way she was sizing him up. I'm so sorry, Halo. So deeply sorry. Are you okay?"

"Not really. I'm sitting here trying to figure out how to find White Wolf's cabin again."

"White Wolf! He can't help you with this."

"No one else can help me with this. I have another matter I need his advice on. Something extraordinary happened this morning. If not for that, I'd be on a flight out of here right now."

"Whoa. Must be major. Can you tell me?"

"Not over the phone. I really have more questions for your father about Feather Blue."

"Where are you?"

"At my storage unit," she replied, staring at the row of rental garages opposite the storage sheds.

"I'll take you up," he said. "Do you have a place to store your car? If not, you can park it at Moss's house."

"I'm facing a row of garage stalls as we speak. I'd rather not leave my car at Moss's but thank you for the offer. Shade and Malika are still on the prowl. And I don't want anyone else knowing my whereabouts."

"I hear ya. Are you at Levi and Moss's storage facility?"

"Yes."

"I'll make sure they don't charge you," he said with kindness in his voice. "I'll get a key from Moss and be over shortly. Do you have a bag packed?"

"No." She sighed. "I haven't had a chance. I'll root through my unit and throw a few things together. What I don't have I can buy on the road. I can't go back to Rush's. I just can't." She held back tears.

"Don't worry, Halo. You don't have to go through this alone. I'm here for you."

"Thank you." She dabbed her eyes and sniffed back tears. "You might wanna tell Ricochet not to waste time trying to rescue Malika. I know you've all been on the fence as to whether she's a victim or not."

"Oh?"

"Trust me. She's no victim. I have shocking news. I was going to tell Rush but when I found him with Camille, I lost my mind."

"Is Malika still on the warpath?" he asked.

"I would say yes. And I really question Camille's motives. But I don't have the mental energy to deal with her again. She's Rush's problem now."

"You shouldn't have to deal with this again. I'm done playing their game. They know I'm a Fed. If Malika or Shade cross my path, I'll haul them both in and they're well aware of it."

"Has Shade committed a crime?"

"Many, but we have no proof. This time, he's abetting a terrorist and could be an accomplice to murder, trafficking, and other crimes. Once we get them in and interrogate them, one of them will break and talk. His confirmed affiliation with Malika, and undisclosed paternity, is enough to bring him in for a closer look. And if Camille's involved, she'll go down with them." Shook paused with a despondent sigh. "I'm sorry you got a shitty family. You deserve much better."

"Don't pity me. There's a ray of sunshine in all this. That's part of what I want to tell you. but I'll wait until you get here."

"Look to your left, babe. I'm here."

She peered out her window. Sure enough, a magnificent silver and black Harley was rumbling into the lot. She smiled a little and tucked her phone away. She was relieved to see a welcome face.

He pulled up to her window. "Moss was more than happy to give us the keys to his nicest garage. Your car will be safe."

"How'd you get here so fast?"

"I stayed at Moss's last night."

She stepped from the car. "I need to grab a few things from my storage. My life feels scattered from Dallas to Denver."

He parked his bike and walked with her. "I wish I knew what to say."

"Sometimes saying nothing is saying the most." She unlocked the unit.

Shook lifted the door for her. "This is the first time I've been personally involved with a woman on the run. Words are harder to find in this situation."

"You must feel torn, being that Rush is your best friend." She rooted through boxes until finding the one labeled EDC.

"Not torn. Disappointed in him. Rush knew the risks, yet he ignored them. And more upsetting is how he dismissed my warnings to help that maneater."

"Maybe he wanted a way out." She filled a backpack with essential items.

"Why would you think that?"

She shrugged. "He made several comments recently. He was growing impatient. Getting frustrated. Having trouble controlling his jealousy."

"Jealousy? Over what?"

Cameo zipped her pack closed and pushed the box back into place. "Rebar . . . and you. He was upset when I wore Rebar's jacket and felt threatened by the Lakota connection you and I share. He had a few issues with me like when I hid the feather and secretly texted Moss to check on Rebar."

"I knew he was upset that I kissed you, but I had no idea he was nitpicking everything else."

"He didn't hide his anger over Rebar hugging me. We were only talking. There was nothing going on. Rush stalked up to us and acted all dominant, accused Rebar of upsetting me. He wasn't nice about it. I was overwhelmed by everything, and Rebar was merely comforting me."

Shook eased her around to look at him. "Is that why you bolted that day?"

She gazed into his black eyes and nodded. "Didn't he tell you?"

"No. He said you needed to blow off some tension. When we checked the weather, he decided to launch a search. He'd have gone looking for you either way, but he didn't seem panicked. Everyone wanted an update and Rush insisted on giving them one before splitting up again. I thought something didn't seem right."

"Just as well," she said. "He quit looking once he found Camille anyway. Sorry I caused more drama for you and the others."

He lifted her chin with a light touch. "You didn't cause anything. And you contacted me the next morning once you calmed down. You've been through hell the past few months. I just happen to have TLC therapy that never fails."

She couldn't withhold a smile. He had that effect on her. "And just what do you have in mind?"

He made a sweeping gesture with one arm toward his impressive Harley. "That's my therapy. Works every time."

"I'm totally up for that." She gazed back up at him. "Will your father mind?"

"White Wolf will be thrilled to see us again, especially you. Have you forgotten what he said?" Shook asked with a beguiling smile.

"Not at all. I fell in love with your father. He's pretty unforgettable," she replied. "What about you? Are you up for another few days on the road?"

"Up for it?" His brows vaulted. "I live for it."

"I think your method of therapy is just what I need. I'll get my baby tucked in so we can be on our way."

He slung her backpack over one shoulder then closed and locked the storage unit. "I'll put this on the bike in the meantime. EDC, huh? Looks like someone has moved around a lot."

"I always keep an Every-Day-Carry bag on hand. My job demands it."

"Forestry and Wildlife, right?"

"I didn't know you knew what I do for a living."

He shrugged modestly. "Job habit. Always paying attention to everyone around me." He gave her a sexy, quirky grin. "And I'm a FED remember? I do my research."

She stared at him for a moment, impressed by his laidback style amidst her personal crisis and during a looming threat to Ricochet. He was as cool and no less hot than Rebar or Rush. All the men of Ricochet were easy on the eyes. But only three had that extra special something going on, and what Cameo called the *cool factor gene*.

She recalled the first time they met and the charming smile he'd greeted her with. Then how he'd casually stretched out on his Harley while they waited to track Missy and Joan. He'd always been on the quiet side and hanging in the background, yet a powerful force all the same.

"Everything okay?" he asked, tilting his head curiously.

"Oh . . . sorry. Got sidetracked there for a minute. Be right back." She practically dived behind the wheel of her car to hide the embarrassment of being caught gawking.

After securing her car in the rented garage, then covering

it, she made sure to lock the doors and the garage door before walking back to Shook. He sat straddling the black leather seat of his bike, patiently waiting.

"Hop on, pretty lady. Let's get some therapy." He gave her a playful wink.

She swung her leg over the back and settled onto the passenger seat, resting her hands at his waist. His Harley had a half-backrest, so she felt secure enough to relax without keeping a tight grip on him. Plus, she'd seen him drive, which gave her complete confidence in riding with him.

"You smell good," she said, noticing his straight black hair was still damp. "What cologne do you wear?"

"I don't wear any." He turned his head halfway. "Just soap, shampoo, and deodorant."

"Mm. Nice mix with the leather jacket. Fresh. Clean." She leaned a bit closer.

"I'm glad you approve," he said with a light laugh. "All settled in back there?"

"Yes, sir. I'm ready to ride." She drew in a deep breath of cool night air laced with his invigorating scent.

They had a long ride ahead of them but this time she saw it as a getaway, not an urgent trip. Though she hoped White Wolf would offer some guidance on the real Feather Blue, she didn't feel pressured to get there in record time. Cameo looked forward to a few more stops along the way and getting to know Shook better.

Without the worry of stirring jealousy from another man, she could focus more on learning about her heritage, her mother, and the land she would soon call home.

She especially looked forward to sharing her good news with Shook, the one person she knew would be happy for her. They shared a spiritual bond and other common factors such as their half-breed status and Native American parents from the same Nation. He had the full-blooded Lakota father, and she had the Lakota mother.

*Thank God we're not related,* she mused. She didn't want to discover any more estranged siblings. Cameo remembered White Wolf's story about his true love Rain Song, the white woman whose parents took her away and left Shook behind.

Though her past and Shook's shared similar threads, they were vastly different. She longed to find Feather Blue and embrace her Native American culture on a deeper level.

Two revelations she was profoundly grateful for, Malika was not her mother and the General not her father. Thank God, not a drop of their blood flowed through her veins, and not a thread of their DNA. She found it hard to stay angry with Jared after pondering his video. He'd taken wrong turns most of his life and ended up in the clutches of evil people, which resulted in never meeting one daughter and handing her twin over to depraved men. She couldn't imagine living with that guilt.

If she were totally honest with herself, the two-hundred acres helped to ease the pain of his failure as a parent.

She'd had every intention of telling Camille but never got the chance thanks to the betrayal. Her sister continued sinking to new levels of treachery that Cameo simply could not accept. She didn't feel optimistic about them ever becoming close. Camille had inherited her fortune from Jared, and Cameo just received hers — an inheritance that held far more value than all the money in the world.

Once the dust settled, perhaps one day they'd reconcile enough for an occasional visit. Her sister needed a man, and some kids to keep her grounded. Though she couldn't imagine her sister as a loving mother. Cameo yearned for her peaceful life again, doing what she loved, taking care of animals and land. And Jared had made that possible . . .

Nevertheless, before any of that could happen, she needed to honor her father's request and find Feather Blue. And she had a feeling that Shook and White Wolf would be a big part of this new journey.

Cameo also liked that she'd live closer to Rebar. She hadn't forgotten about him. But those feelings had to be placed on hold for now, especially with Camille on the loose. The woman might decide she wanted both Damocles men.

*I know all too well what it feels like to be in the middle . . . Rebar, Camille . . . now Rush. And that's an F5 twister I want to avoid.*

Read what happens next in Feather Blue: Book 9

# ABOUT THE AUTHOR

Shiloh is a bookworm who grew into an author. Writing has been a way of life for her since grade school. In her words, "The only time I'm truly free is when I'm writing."

As a survivor of hardship and chronic disease, she takes one day at a time and treasures the simple things in life. Shiloh is a Christian, loves animals and practices being kind and generous every day.

Her achievements include The Golden Wings Award for her debut novel The Satellite, the UK Nobel Pin and Editor's Choice Award for her poem The Lonely Man, numerous 5 Star Reviews from Fallen Angels Reviews, InD'tale Magazine, and other professional reviewers for novels published under former pen names.

Her novel Forever in Darkness became a finalist in the 2017 RONE Awards.

Her novel *Chained Reaction* earned her third 5 Star Crowned Heart Review and a nomination for the RONE 2021 Awards.

*Writing stories you'll live in!*

www.SusanZoeBella.com